D01922259

Readers love
ANDREW GREY

The Best Worst Honeymoon Ever

"…in his usual deft manner, Grey leads the reader through it all and still leaves that sense of romance and hope that seem to follow in all his books. This is a great and fun summer read."

—Paranormal Romance Guild

"…if you're looking for a read full of gentle loving, great scenery, amazing excursions and wildlife, and a perfect happy ending, then you will probably love this novel as much as I do."

—Rainbow Book Reviews

Redeeming the Stepbrother

"God, I loved this! When done well, modern fairy tales make wonderful reads. Andrew Grey certainly does this well, and Redeeming the Stepbrother was a joy."

—Joyfully Jay

"I recommend this story to all those who love fairytales and literary works based on them. This series is a good one and I can't wait to see which tale comes next."

—The Novel Approach

By ANDREW GREY

Accompanied by a Waltz
All for You
Between Loathing and Love
Borrowed Heart
Buried Passions
Chasing the Dream
Crossing Divides
Dominant Chord
Dutch Treat
Eastern Cowboy
In Search of a Story
New Tricks
Noble Intentions
North to the Future
One Good Deed
The Playmaker
Running to You
Saving Faithless Creek
Shared Revelations
Three Fates
To Have, Hold, and Let Go
Turning the Page
Whipped Cream

ART
Legal Artistry • Artistic Appeal
Artistic Pursuits • Legal Tender

BOTTLED UP
The Best Revenge • Bottled Up
Uncorked • An Unexpected Vintage

BRONCO'S BOYS
Inside Out • Upside Down
Backward • Round and Round

THE BULLRIDERS
A Wild Ride • A Daring Ride • A Courageous Ride

BY FIRE
Redemption by Fire • Strengthened by Fire
Burnished by Fire • Heat Under Fire

CARLISLE COPS
Fire and Water • Fire and Ice • Fire and Rain
Fire and Snow • Fire and Hail • Fire and Fog

CARLISLE DEPUTIES
Fire and Flint • Fire and Granite

Published by DREAMSPINNER PRESS
www.dreamspinnerpress.com

By ANDREW GREY

CHEMISTRY
Organic Chemistry • Biochemistry •
Electrochemistry
Chemistry Anthology

DREAMSPUN DESIRES
#4 – The Lone Rancher
#28 – Poppy's Secret
#60 – The Best Worst Honeymoon Ever

EYES OF LOVE
Eyes Only for Me • Eyes Only for You

FOREVER YOURS
Can't Live Without You •
Never Let You Go

GOOD FIGHT
The Good Fight • The Fight Within
The Fight for Identity •
Takoda and Horse

HEARTS ENTWINED
Heart Unseen • Heart Unheard

HOLIDAY STORIES
Copping a Sweetest Day Feel • Cruise for Christmas
A Lion in Tails • Mariah the Christmas Moose
A Present in Swaddling Clothes • Simple Gifts
Snowbound in Nowhere • Stardust

LAS VEGAS ESCORTS
The Price • The Gift

LOVE MEANS…
Love Means… No Shame •
Love Means… Courage
Love Means… No Boundaries • Love Means… Freedom
Love Means … No Fear •
Love Means… Healing
Love Means… Family •
Love Means… Renewal
Love Means… No Limits •
Love Means… Patience
Love Means… Endurance

LOVE'S CHARTER
Setting the Hook • Ebb and Flow

Published by DREAMSPINNER PRESS
www.dreamspinnerpress.com

By ANDREW GREY

PLANTING DREAMS
Planting His Dream • Growing His Dream

REKINDLED FLAME
Rekindled Flame • Cleansing Flame
Smoldering Flame

SENSES
Love Comes Silently • Love Comes in Darkness
Love Comes Home • Love Comes Around
Love Comes Unheard • Love Comes to Light

SEVEN DAYS
Seven Days • Unconditional Love

STORIES FROM THE RANGE
A Shared Range • A Troubled Range • An Unsettled Range
A Foreign Range • An Isolated Range
A Volatile Range • A Chaotic Range

STRANDED
Stranded • Taken

TALES FROM KANSAS
Dumped in Oz • Stuck in Oz • Trapped in Oz

TALES FROM ST. GILES
Taming the Beast • Redeeming the Stepbrother

TASTE OF LOVE
A Taste of Love • A Serving of Love
A Helping of Love • A Slice of Love

WITHOUT BORDERS
A Heart Without Borders • A Spirit Without Borders

WORK OUT
Spot Me • Pump Me Up • Core Training
Crunch Time • Positive Resistance
Personal Training • Cardio Conditioning
Work Me Out Anthology

Published by DREAMSPINNER PRESS
www.dreamspinnerpress.com

Published by
DREAMSPINNER PRESS

5032 Capital Circle SW, Suite 2, PMB# 279,
Tallahassee, FL 32305-7886 USA
www.dreamspinnerpress.com
This is a work of fiction. Names, characters, places, and incidents either are the product of author imagination or are used fictitiously, and any resemblance to actual persons, living or dead, business establishments, events, or locales is entirely coincidental.

Borrowed Heart
© 2019 Andrew Grey.

Cover Art
© 2019 Adrian Nicholas
adrian.nicholas177@gmail.com
Cover content is for illustrative purposes only and any person depicted on the cover is a model.

All rights reserved. This book is licensed to the original purchaser only. Duplication or distribution via any means is illegal and a violation of international copyright law, subject to criminal prosecution and upon conviction, fines, and/or imprisonment. Any eBook format cannot be legally loaned or given to others. No part of this book may be reproduced or transmitted in any form or by any means, electronic or mechanical, including photocopying, recording, or by any information storage and retrieval system, without the written permission of the Publisher, except where permitted by law. To request permission and all other inquiries, contact Dreamspinner Press, 5032 Capital Circle SW, Suite 2, PMB# 279, Tallahassee, FL 32305-7886, USA, or www.dreamspinnerpress.com.

Mass Market Paperback ISBN: 978-1-64108-137-5
Trade Paperback ISBN: 978-1-64080-825-6
Digital ISBN: 978-1-64080-824-9
Library of Congress Control Number: 2018943364
Mass Market Paperback published March 2019
v. 1.0

Printed in the United States of America
∞
This paper meets the requirements of
ANSI/NISO Z39.48-1992 (Permanence of Paper).

To Dominic, for all his help with
the German travel details.

CHAPTER 1

LEAD. IT felt like a hunk of lead pressed down on his chest. What the hell it was there for, he had no idea.

Robin cracked his eyes open. A cat sat in the middle of his chest, blinking slowly at him.

"Schnitzel. What are you doing here?" Robin groaned, remembering he'd left the window open again. God, had he had that much to drink last night that he couldn't remember getting into bed? Robin sat up, and Schnitzel jumped down and raced away. Though the old boy was the neighbor's cat, he acted like he owned the place. He must have gotten out again. Poor Mrs. Kleindinst must be worried sick.

"You don't live here," Robin said as the cat stopped just outside the sleeping area, blinking at him as though Robin were stupid. Maybe he was. Robin certainly needed to remember to stop at two glasses of wine. His mouth felt like someone had filled it with cotton and poured glue in to make sure it stayed that way for a damn long time.

He walked around the screen that created his bedroom and out into the "everything else" area of his tiny Frankfurt apartment. Not that it bothered him. He could afford it, and the amount of space didn't really matter so much because he was rarely there.

Schnitzel yowled to voice his displeasure, and Robin scooped him up. Schnitzel turned to him, blinking a few times, doing his best to look pathetic and hungry. It didn't work. The gray-and-white tiger cat weighed fifteen pounds and usually ate better than Robin.

Still in his sleep pants and T-shirt, Robin carried Schnitzel across the hall and knocked quietly on the door. Mrs. K cracked it open, and Robin pushed the cat into her line of sight. She gasped and opened the door, filling the hallway with rapid-fire concern and even a touch of embarrassment in Frankish, a German dialect Robin still struggled to understand.

"You come in. Have breakfast," she said in heavily accented English. "You need. Too much beer." She smiled, and Robin seriously considered taking her up on her offer. She was supremely kind to him, seeming to have adopted him in a way. Mrs. K didn't have family as far as Robin could tell, or they never visited, which was even sadder as far as he was concerned.

"I have to work today," he said in High German, and she nodded, patting his cheek gently. "I'll bring you some chocolate."

She smiled. Mrs. K had a real love of chocolate, so he always brought her back something unusual from his various tours.

Robin padded back to his apartment, closed the door, and then stripped off his clothes. He squeezed into his tiny bathroom and ran water in the tub for a shallow bath.

Twenty minutes later, he was dressed and had packed his things in a single, rather small bag. He'd gotten used to packing light. After all, he wasn't the one on vacation. His basic work wardrobe of tan pants and a blue or white shirt with the Euro Pride Tours logo on the front didn't take much space. Whether seven or eleven days, it was all pretty much the same. His extra shoes took up more space than anything else.

Robin checked the clock and instantly wished he'd taken Mrs. K up on her offer. He prepared the apartment to be empty for a week and a half, turned off all the appliances, and made sure there was nothing perishable anywhere. Then he grabbed his jacket, locked the door, and walked down to the train station.

"YOU MADE it," Albert said as Robin entered the office, dragging his bag behind him as though it weighed a million pounds.

"Yeah. I almost called and told you to find someone else." He set the bag behind the desk and flopped down into one of the chairs Albert reserved for customers, but he didn't care. "The train broke down in one of the tunnels." Robin swore under his breath.

"I heard about that," Albert said, glaring but not asking Robin to move. There was no one in the office but them. "I have the details on your group." Albert handed him a packet of information. "This one is mostly Americans. That's why I gave it to you. Hopefully they won't notice the grumps you've had for the last six months." He flitted around behind his desk and sat. "What's with you anyway? People go on vacation to be happy and have fun, not be led by Oscar the Grouch."

He smiled at his own little joke. "It's your job to make sure they have fun."

Robin humphed. This wasn't the first time they'd had this conversation. "I know. My groups always have fun." And they did; Robin worked very hard to make sure of that.

"Yeah, but when you think they aren't watching, you…." Albert looked at Robin with his big cow eyes and wild blond hair, the epitome of style and fun. "Well, you look like that." He pointed and waved his hands. "All scrunched up and sad. It's depressing."

"When was the last time you got dumped?" Robin asked as he looked over the paperwork. Americans. God. Why couldn't he have a nice group of British tourists? They were always so pleasant and usually wanted a no-stress, relaxing holiday. Robin craved people like that. Americans wanted to go, go, go and be entertained every second of the day. He sighed and closed the folder. At least this was a mixed group and not all gay men—sometimes that helped.

"I never get dumped. I do the dumping when they get all clingy and needy and shit." Albert batted his lashes, and Robin could see why. Guys would come running for his lithe little body and amazing eyes. He was German, but he'd spent years in the US, so he spoke English very well and loved Americanisms. "You need to give it a try."

"What?" Robin looked up from the itinerary he'd been reading.

"Haven't you been listening?" Albert asked testily. "I was saying that you need to get over whoever this guy was and get on with it." He rolled his eyes like the drama queen he was. "Whoever this guy was… is… whatever… you kicked him to the curb, so find another one to make your engine purr." He actually rumbled like some huge cat, and it was Robin's turn to roll his eyes. "And not me."

Robin nearly fell out of the chair. "Please. You think every guy wants you."

"And most of them do. I work hard to keep things in top condition." Albert stood, walked to the door, and turned like he was a model on a runway. He had style, there was no doubt about it, and he could play the young party boy even as he looked on in fear as forty approached the horizon. He sat back down, the chair rolling a little as he did. "Enough about all this. Let's talk about this tour, shall we?"

"It's what I live for," Robin retorted, and Albert smiled.

"That's the spirit. Be funny. People like that." He typed at his computer, and Robin tried to figure out what he'd done that was funny.

"What's this?" Robin asked, pointing to the sheet. "I have someone joining the tour late?"

"You might. I have someone—he's in Germany for a while—who was interested in the tour. He was going to join you in Würzburg Thursday evening. We don't normally do that, but there's space and, well…." Albert waved his hand, but Robin already knew the answer. Albert wasn't going to turn down business, no matter what his own policies were. Money talked, and everything else was secondary. It was how Albert had managed to stay in business as a small tour operator when everyone else was either gobbled up by the big operations or simply went away.

"All right. How will I know this guy?" Robin asked, grabbing a pen to make notes.

"I'm waiting on his payment, which he was going to call in today. If he makes it, then he'll meet you at the hotel where dinner is booked, so everyone will be there. He'll ask for you. It shouldn't be a problem. Just make sure he has a copy of my email, and everything will be fine." Albert continued typing while they talked, and Robin jotted down the information.

"Okay. Is there anything else I need to know?"

Albert shook his head, already getting sucked into his work and forgetting about nearly anything else. "Just make sure they have a good time. These are gay tours, so for God's sake, keep the *gay* in them. Make them happy. Take them to clubs in the evening. You have the list of the ones we work with. Just show them a good time. Think of yourself as a party planner as well as a tour guide." Albert lifted his hands away from the keyboard, rocking to some music that only he could hear.

Robin groaned inwardly. He'd taken this job because he thought it would give him a chance to get his feet under him again. His mom and dad wanted nothing more than for him to fly back to Milwaukee and tend the bar in the family German restaurant—just what he wanted to do for the rest of his life. Not that he was all that much happier with what he was doing now, but at least he was on his own and taking advantage of his dual citizenship.

"I have never planned parties. But I get your point and I'll try." He managed a smile. "When is everyone arriving?"

"They'll start getting here any time now. The bus will arrive at eleven."

"Who is the driver?" Robin asked. "It isn't that Romanian guy who nearly killed us all, is it?" That had been a near disaster—no pun intended. Yuri had stayed up all night for some reason, and he'd fallen asleep behind the wheel and nearly driven them all off a cliff. Robin had taken over driving as well as guiding the group for the last two days.

"No. I fired him. Your driver is Johan. He worked with you a few months ago, and to my surprise was willing to do it again." Albert turned away, half hiding behind his computer screen. The coward.

"What's with that crap? I'm always good to my drivers." Robin glared at Albert, who had the decency to blush a little. He was nice to them all, even Johan, who reminded Robin of Cousin Itt, with his loose hair nearly down to his butt and a thick black beard that would make Hagrid proud.

"Yes, you make sure they are treated nicely, but you're so dang depressed all the time. Poor Dieter, your last driver, is on a vacation of his own so he could get some sunshine and happiness. People do this job because it's fun and makes them feel good. They want to be happy. You're like a big, huge ball of sad." Albert made a face like he'd just sucked a lemon. "So for God's sake, try to be happy. Take some pills if you have to, please. You can't keep going like this."

"Fine." Robin grinned and stood to wander to the window. "I'll be perky, chipper, and a bundle of happiness."

Albert pushed away from his desk. "Don't go too far. I don't want your head to explode. Just show them a good time and try to have one yourself. This is a great itinerary. You're going to the baths in Baden-Baden, so take the time to go in yourself, get a massage." Albert grinned wickedly. "Take Johan in with you and get him to give you a massage." He fanned his face dramatically. "Just have fun, okay?"

"Yeah." Robin figured he could fake it for eleven days. Things couldn't be that bad, and it was time he pulled his sorry ass out of the funk he'd been in. It was either that or go home and help his parents in the restaurant. "I'll do my best." Robin grabbed his folder and left the office, the outside door whooshing closed behind him as people began approaching.

"Euro Pride Tours?" asked a huge young man with testosterone rolling off him. An older man approached behind him, pulling a large suitcase on wheels. The young guy rolled his eyes, set his own suitcase aside, hurried back, and took the older man's bag. "Come on, Oliver." He lifted the suitcase as though it weighed nothing, looking like he was about to burst out of the überthin, skintight shirt that showed every ripple of muscle. "Everything is going to be fine. This is the place."

"Then why did we have to walk eight blocks in the wrong direction first?" Oliver complained as he approached the office, breathing deeply.

Oliver was white-haired and pale, even kind of frail-looking, whereas his companion was young, virile, tanned, and toned. Oliver wore a silk shirt that flowed and shimmered in the light breeze. His pants were linen, flowing over his thin legs, and the rings on his fingers sparkled in the sunlight. He clearly had money, and his partner… well, it didn't take much imagination to understand the basic dynamics of their relationship.

"This is Javier Montel, and I'm Oliver Justinian," he told those already assembled.

Javier stepped closer to Oliver, putting an arm around his waist to show they were together.

"I'm Robin Fuller, and it's a pleasure to meet both of you." He shook their hands. "The bus will be here about eleven," Robin explained as he ticked their names off his list and gave them both a boarding ticket. "If you like, you can go inside. There are a few chairs. Tag your luggage with these." He handed over plastic rainbow luggage tags to both of them, and Oliver handed his to Javier immediately. "You can put your luggage against the building. I'll stay out here to wait for more of our group."

"Go on inside and sit down, Oliver," Javier said. "I'm going to stay out here in the sunshine." He smiled, and Oliver shared a look with Javier that Robin wished he hadn't seen. Then he went inside and sat down.

"Are you looking forward to your vacation?" Robin asked.

Javier stood away from the building on the sidewalk, looking up at the sky as the sun broke through the clouds. He was a stunning-looking man, and Robin turned away to review more of the folder. "Another day…." He shrugged, then stood still.

Robin read the last of the details as a group of people approached. "Euro Pride Tours," he said, and the group all smiled and nodded.

A tall man in his midtwenties approached and shook Robin's hand enthusiastically. "Grant Harcourt."

"I'm Robin Fuller." He managed to pull his hand away before Grant shook his arm off. "Excellent. You can put your luggage there until the bus comes."

Grant stepped closer, still vibrating with excitement. "Will you be giving us a tour of Frankfurt?" He looked all around as though fascinated.

"No. Frankfurt was nearly completely destroyed during the war, and there is little of historical interest left." Robin turned to address the group. "Once the bus arrives—" He checked his watch. "—which should be soon, we'll get set and boarded, and we'll go directly to Würzburg."

"Oh, okay." Grant fished a guidebook out of his worn messenger bag, opened it, and leaned against the building to read. Robin left him to it and turned to a pair of young men about college age.

"Kyle North and Billy Thomas." The taller of the two spoke for both of them, pointing as he said their names.

Robin gave them their tags and boarding tickets.

"Luggage over there?" Kyle asked, turning to the others. "He and I are best friends," Kyle overexplained as he looked at Javier with barely disguised interest. Oliver came out and joined Javier, slipping an arm around his waist. Kyle turned away and talked with Billy.

This was definitely going to be an interesting group.

Two other couples joined them, Mary and Helen from Indianapolis, and Harold and Gerald from Texas. They joined the rest of the growing group of people, talking excitedly about their tour and what they hoped to see.

A voice carried across the sound of traffic, followed by a blaring bus horn. Robin looked up as their bus lurched to a stop for two women racing across the street.

"I told you to get up earlier."

"I thought we'd have plenty of time." The women hurried up to where Robin stood as the bus pulled in. "Lily Martin," one woman said with a nervous smile. "This is my friend Margaret Hansen." Lily played with her nails nervously.

"Welcome, ladies." Robin handed them their tags as the tour bus pulled to a stop beside their group. "The driver will load the luggage when he's done parking." Robin checked over his group. They seemed nice enough and excited—well, all but Lily, who stood near Margaret almost defensively.

"I don't know why we had to go on a gay tour," Lily said just loud enough that Robin was able to hear.

"Because I'm a lesbian, and you said you wanted a nice, relaxing vacation without men. Well…." Margaret motioned around her.

Robin turned away, smiling to himself. Okay, maybe he could be happy, or at the very least, less depressed and sad all the damn time. So he'd gotten dumped after five years. It was time to move on and get over it. He stood waiting until Johan had the bus parked, soaking in some of the energy of his tourists.

The bus farted, which was what it always sounded like to Robin when the brakes released. Thankfully this was the smaller kind of bus that held about twenty people when fully loaded, though there was still plenty of space for everyone in the group to spread out. No wonder Albert had taken the extra fare. There was room, and he was paying for the bus, driver, and Robin, no matter how many people there were.

"All right. Johan will load the luggage, and I'll check everyone in as you get on the bus. Then we can go."

The group all gathered around him, with a few grumbles that they should have gotten something to eat first. Robin, prepared for that, pulled granola bars out of his bag and passed them out.

The bus door opened, and Johan stepped out. Robin's mouth went dry and he looked longer than was necessary, but he couldn't help it. Gone was Cousin Itt with the beard and superlong hair. Hello clean-shaven, black hair flowing down to his shoulders, god among men. Robin had no idea what the hell had happened, but one thing was for certain: all the guys, and Lily, turned and gaped as Johan strode off the bus.

"Are you ready for me?" he asked in a soft voice, and it took Robin a second to get his mind out of the gutter.

Robin nodded and swallowed once again. "All the luggage is tagged and ready to be loaded." He pointed to the line of bags, and Johan nodded, walking over to heft two bags to the bus and load them into the luggage compartment underneath. Robin turned away from where Johan worked and stood by the door to the bus. No one moved, the guys enthralled by Johan, watching him work. Robin cleared his throat, and they seemed to come back from whatever fantasies had gripped them. Not that Robin didn't understand. He suddenly found himself with his own fantasies, and they weren't professional in the least.

One by one, Robin checked off each of his tour members as they got on the bus. Javier got on first, half leaping into the bus, then pausing at the top with a sigh as Oliver climbed in more slowly. The ladies all followed, and then the others filed on, with Kyle and Billy bringing up the rear, chatting a mile a minute.

"Will we be stopping at any clubs and things?" Kyle asked, Robin repressing a smile as Billy rolled his eyes from behind Kyle.

"We have plenty of free time for things like that. Robin doesn't have to act like a wingman." Billy zipped past Kyle and got on the bus.

Kyle shook his head and followed.

"Is that everyone?" Johan asked from where he stood near the luggage compartment.

"Yes." Robin sighed. "We might have another joining us in Würzburg tomorrow evening."

Johan nodded and closed the luggage door.

"Shoot," Robin muttered and hurried into the office. He grabbed his own suitcase, then returned. Johan took the bag, his fingers brushing lightly over Robin's, sending heat along his skin. Robin pulled back more quickly than was necessary. Hopefully Johan hadn't noticed. "Now we can go." Robin followed Johan onto the bus and they were off.

"Guten Morgen. I'm Robin, and I'm going to be your tour guide for the next eleven days. I'm sure you're all familiar with the itinerary, and as far as I know, there aren't any changes that we are expecting. Our driver, Johan—" He paused, and Johan waved quickly before merging into traffic. "—and I will be here to make sure you get where you need to. At any time during the trip, I will be happy to answer questions. Now, for most of our day trips, Johan will lock the bus, so you can feel free to leave your things in the overhead compartment, or we can put them in the locked compartments."

"Even my laptop?" Grant asked, his hand shooting in the air.

"Yes. Your laptops, sweaters, jackets… all of it. We don't recommend that you leave things on the bus overnight, because Johan will need to park it and he'll be at the hotel with us." Robin gazed out at the faces all looking back at him expectantly. "The drive to Würzburg is going to take about two hours with traffic, so I thought I'd give you a little overview of the country we're going to be seeing. The country we know as Germany didn't always look the way it does today. Up until a hundred and fifty or so years ago, it was many different sovereign states—Prussia, Franconia, and Bavaria, to name a few of them. They each had their own rulers and royal lines. You may have heard of some of them."

"What about East Germany? Was that one of them?" Billy asked, and Kyle nudged him sharply.

"No. That's because of the war," Kyle interjected.

"What we know or knew as East and West Germany resulted from World War II. East Germany was the part controlled by the Russians. Germany was reunified in 1990." Robin took a deep breath and continued. "We are going to see palaces, castles, and Roman ruins, taste wine…."

"And get drunk…," a couple said together, and everyone laughed.

Robin tried to laugh along with them, but failed, waiting them out instead. Kyle and Billy started talking about beer, and the conversation took off on its own. Popping and hissing sounds followed, and both Kyle and Billy sipped from cans, offering them to others as well. Soon almost everyone was drinking, and Robin wondered how they'd gotten that much beer on the bus right under his nose. He was going to have to keep an eye on those two. Giving up on imparting any more information, he sat down and let the group talk while they rode.

"It is okay," Johan said from just in front of him. "They need to get to know one another, and this is a good time for them to do it."

"I suppose. I usually have get-to-know-each-other games," Robin explained, and Johan snorted. "What?"

"I remember those games. The beer is better." He returned to his driving, chuckling under his breath. Robin wanted to smack him, but as he turned to look at the rest of the group, he had to agree that the beer was better. They were having a good time, talking and laughing. Robin faced forward, watching the road and scenery out the front window as they entered the Autobahn. He opened the file and reviewed it once again, needing something to do.

AS THEY approached the outskirts of Würzburg, Robin stood up, holding on to his seat back. "As we come into town, we're going to park near the restaurant for lunch. Then you'll have the afternoon to look around. At four, we'll meet at the hotel to check in and have dinner. The evening is on your own, and tomorrow we have a guided tour of the town and the Würzburg Residence, the Prince-Bishop's palace, which is truly amazing."

"Should we take our things with us?" Javier asked.

"Take your handheld things. The rest will be safe until we get to the hotel. It's a short walk to town from the bus park, so you probably don't want to trek back."

Johan parked the bus in the lot and turned off the engine, and Robin got off the bus, directing everyone into the nearby restaurant.

"Lock up the bus and join us."

Johan nodded. "Save me a seat?" He smiled, and Robin's belly did a little flip of excitement.

"Sure." He grabbed his bag and left the bus, walking briskly to catch up.

Inside the restaurant, he gave the hostess their information, and they were seated at a long table against the far dark-paneled wall. Soon drinks and salads were brought out, followed by plates of schnitzel with fries. Robin made sure everyone was seated and had food before taking his place at the one end. Johan came in and sat at the other end of the table, where a plate waited for him.

"How long have you been driving buses for tours?" Grant asked from next to Johan.

"About four years," Johan answered, his accent a little thicker than it had been earlier. Maybe Johan was a little shy when it came to talking about himself?

"How old is this town?" Kyle asked.

Johan set down his fork and swallowed but didn't get a chance to answer.

"The first cathedral was built in 788 and it was consecrated by Charlemagne. The current one dates to the eleventh century. So the town is over 1300 years old at least." Grant sounded like one of the tour guidebooks he'd been reading.

Robin took over when Grant ran out of steam. "It's beautiful, with buildings of all styles. Take a walk through the cathedral—it's breathtaking. Germany's most famous wood-carver, Tilman Riemenschneider, was also the mayor of the town. So you'll see plenty of his work. Look for pieces in the cathedral itself. Otherwise, look through the shops and markets. Enjoy yourselves and be at the hotel between four and five to get your rooms."

"Where is it?"

"The Hotel Charlemagne is just down the street toward town, about two blocks from here," Robin explained. "If you walk into town, you can't miss it. Have fun for a few hours."

They all finished their lunches, and the tourists left the restaurant in small groups until only Robin and Johan remained with Lily and Margaret, who sat at the other end of the table, speaking quietly. Then after a few minutes, they stood as well.

Robin pulled out the chair next to him. "You can join us if you'd like. We're just finishing up."

"We wanted to see some things, but…."

Lily and Margaret moved closer and sat across from Johan.

"Is there something I can help you with?" Robin asked.

"I didn't know this was a gay tour, and…." She leaned closer and lowered her voice. "Margaret thought I understood, but I didn't know, and I feel really out of place." She reached for a napkin and wiped her eyes.

"You know no one is going to mind at all," Johan said, and Robin nodded his agreement.

"But I'm not gay," she said softly. "What if I do something wrong?"

Margaret put her arm around her friend to comfort her. "I'm sorry. I thought you knew. I booked a tour so you wouldn't have men bothering you." Margaret met Robin's gaze with steel in hers. This was a strong person. "She and her husband—"

"Margie," Lily said softly.

"There's nothing he can do to you now. You know that." Margaret held her tighter. "Do you think I'd let that ass get within a hundred feet of you?" Robin supposed that was Margaret's way of comforting and it seemed to work, surprisingly. "Her husband…."

"He cheated," Lily said and sniffed. "A lot."

"This is a safe place," Robin said. It sounded lame to him, but it was true. "You don't need to worry about any of us. You're safe, and gay or not, we've got your back." Damn, this wasn't the way he wanted to start the tour.

A server approached the table, and Robin asked for a glass of water. She brought it and continued on her way, and Robin passed it to Lily.

"What do you want to do?"

"Kick the bastard in the nuts and…." She drank from the glass and wiped her face. "I think I want to get out of here and have some fun."

"That's the spirit," Margaret told her. "Don't let the ass win." She got up, and Lily did as well. "Let's go see some fun stuff."

Lily nodded, and Robin watched them both go, feeling like shit. He sat at the table for a while, resting. There was plenty of time, and he knew he needed to take advantage of a couple hours of quiet. Robin pulled out a paperback, ordered another drink, and let the group explore a little and get to know each other on their first day.

"Are you ready to go to the hotel?" Johan asked, and Robin realized he'd been lost in his own thoughts and wondered if he'd been staring at something embarrassing instead of his book. As he feared, from where his gaze seemed to have drifted to Johan's chest and the way it filled out his shirt so… completely.

"Yes." Robin pushed back his chair and verified with the hostess that the charges had been covered. Then he and Johan went back to the bus. He sat, watching out the front window, as Johan slowly navigated the bus through the narrow street and up to the front of the hotel.

It was a family-run place. The last time Robin had stayed here on a tour, the couple's fourteen-year-old son had actually checked them in. The half-timbered exterior was exactly what he thought of when he imagined a German hotel. The inside was as quaint and, well, as old-fashioned as the exterior. Not that there was anything wrong with that. It just didn't always meet the expectations that some Americans had for their European holiday.

"Guten Tag," the lady behind the counter said, then smiled. "Robin, you are back."

"Yes," he said, delighted that she remembered him. "I need to get the room keys for my tour group." He handed her the sheet with the details, and she looked it over, nodded, and handed him the keys in an envelope.

"You stay two days?" she asked, and Robin nodded.

"We have one more person joining us tomorrow," he explained, and she nodded as she checked her book.

"We're full tonight, but, *ja*, I can give you the key then." She smiled again, and Robin returned it.

He then sat down with his sheets and keys to make sure everyone got what they paid for. The deluxe room was easy—Oliver had paid for that. It had its own full bath and a small sitting area. The other rooms he assigned and came to the end with only one room left. Robin checked again and groaned. He pulled out his phone to send Albert a message, and received a reply that the number of rooms was incorrect.

"What's up?" Johan said as he carried in the last of the luggage, placing it in the currently unused breakfast room.

"We're a room short," Robin said. "It looks like you and I will have to share." Robin wondered if Albert had planned things like that for the entire tour.

"Okay. It is no big deal," Johan said, and left without another word.

Robin gaped and then pulled his attention back to his records and off Johan's retreating ass. Groaning, Robin wiped his face, then reviewed the room arrangements again, making sure the room he and Johan were in had two beds. Not that he'd mind sharing a bed with Johan, but they worked together, and….

Robin rolled his eyes at himself for the thought. He knew he wasn't the most handsome guy on the planet, and his ex had certainly made that clear in their last conversation-slash-fight, so it only followed that, gay or not, Johan wasn't going to be interested in him. There were certainly guys on this tour who were better-looking and a lot more fun than he was. That was, if Johan was into guys and got involved with the people he drove, and…. Jesus, even his thoughts were rambling. He needed to put a stop to it.

His phone vibrated, finally pulling him out of his circular-running thoughts, and he pulled it out, expecting it to be Albert, but it definitely wasn't. "Hey, Mom," he said with as much happiness as he could muster.

"You're alive," she teased.

"I called last week, and I'm on a tour right now, but everything is fine," he rushed to reassure her, maybe too quickly.

"Are you sure?" she asked, and Robin groaned.

"Yes. I'm taking my pills and watching what I eat as best I can. I always do." He kept his voice light. After years of his mother taking care of him, worrying over him, and then coddling him, or trying to as he got older, he should be used to this routine by now.

"I worry. Why can't you come home? We love you, and you can work with your father and me. Your dad is always saying that he wants to slow down, and if you came into the business, then he could pass some of what he does to you."

"I know you worry, but I'm fine." Robin spoke softly so he wouldn't be overheard. "Really. I like it here, and I get to see parts of the world I never could otherwise. And I get to use my language skills."

His mother cleared her throat nervously. "But what are you doing? Leading tourists around when you could be here with your family where we could help look after you?" Old habits were hard to drop, and his mother was finding letting go extremely difficult.

"I need to be on my own. I've told you that." So much of his life had involved his mother watching him like a hawk, getting ready to rush him to the hospital at the first sign of a cough or fever. Robin had been surprised when his mother had let him actually have a boyfriend. Both his parents had been supportive and caring. That wasn't the surprising part. They had both backed off during the relationship. But as soon as it had ended, they'd returned with the same nearly intrusive care, just like before. "Just let me be. I call, I stay in touch, and I can take care of myself."

She sighed loudly, followed by a small whimper. "You're special, and you can't do all the things other people can. You know that." Robin could imagine her wiping her eyes. "You have to be careful, and I worry about you all the way over there without anyone looking after you."

Robin rubbed the back of his neck, glancing around to make sure no one was listening. "You've told me all this before, and yes, I know that I'm probably not going to live as long as most other people. But I want to have a good life and enjoy what I do have." And unfortunately for his parents, that didn't mean his sitting behind the counter of the family restaurant, taking people's money, spending the rest of his life perched on a stool so his family would know where he was. "I don't know why you're so wound up all of a sudden."

His mother heaved another sigh, and Robin waited for some sort of explanation, but none was forthcoming.

His mom would wait out an ice age if she wanted to, and she clearly didn't intend to spill whatever was bothering her.

"Mom, I need to go. I have to finish getting my tour checked into the hotel, see them to dinner, and then I can rest for the night." He could almost feel his energy being sapped away by this conversation. Not that he didn't love his mother—he did, truly, and Robin knew she loved him a great deal. But being on his own was what he needed so very much. "I'll call you later in the week, and we can text if you want."

She groaned. "You know I can never use that thing." His mother and technology didn't seem to go together.

"Maybe if you let Dad get you a new phone," Robin offered.

"But then I'd have a new number and no one would be able to call, and I'd have to tell everyone and…." She went on, and Robin waited until she wound down a little.

"You can keep the same number," Robin told her, and she paused. "You'd also have an easy way to send messages, instead of using that old flip phone."

"All this new stuff—"

"I know, but it works, and Dad could show you how to use it. You and I could even FaceTime and talk using the camera. Then you could see me." Maybe that would be enough of an incentive. "I have to go and get back to work. It's later here than it is there. You have a good day, and I'll talk to you soon."

"Okay, I love you." She sniffed, and Robin hesitated to let her go.

"I love you too, Mom." Robin hung up and put his phone back in his pocket, and while he was thinking about it, he rummaged in his bag, pulled out a small bottle of water, and took his afternoon pills, then drank the rest of the water and threw the bottle in the recycling bin in the corner.

Oliver and Javier joined him in the lobby. "Is our room ready?" Oliver asked, looking a little worse for wear as he fanned himself.

Javier stood behind him. "You're fine, Ollie. Just a little warm."

Robin got his last bottle of water and handed it to Oliver, who grasped it gratefully and then downed it all.

"I guess I wasn't expecting it to be so warm."

Robin handed him his key. "Johan brought in the bags." He motioned behind them. "You can get settled and relax if you'd like. Dinner is at seven in the same place we had lunch." He smiled, and they left, with Javier loaded down with all the bags.

One by one, the others returned and hauled their luggage up the stairs. By the time everyone had checked in and he had answered half a million questions, Robin realized he only had an hour until dinner. He was tired already and feeling a little run-down.

"I got the bags," Johan said, carrying both of them.

Robin led the way to their room. There were two beds, one double and a tiny cot that looked about as sturdy as a three-legged chair. Robin sighed and opened the window for fresh air as Johan set down the bags.

"Do you want me to see if there is a different room?"

"There isn't," Robin said. "The hotel is full." He looked over at the cot and then at Johan. "Go ahead and take the bed. I'll be fine." He rolled his suitcase next to the cot and sat on the far side of the bed. God, he wanted to lie down and rest for fifteen minutes. At least their room had its own bathroom.

"Are you sure?" Johan asked.

"Yes." There was nothing Robin could do about it. It wasn't like he was going to ask one of his tourists to change rooms so one of them could sleep on the cot. "I'm going to clean up and get ready for dinner."

AFTER DINNER, the group had taken a night tour of the town. Most of them had settled in a small café near the town center for coffee and dessert. Robin made sure they knew their way back to the hotel and then went back himself. He needed to try to get some sleep.

He unlocked the room and stepped in, just as Johan came out of the bathroom, a small towel around his waist that barely covered his bits and butt, leaving strong legs and sexy abs exposed to Robin's hungry gaze. He turned away and went right to his bag, busying himself as Johan moved behind him, hopefully dressing.

"Are you going out?" Johan asked.

"No. Most of the group found a café. Billy and Kyle went off to find some nightlife." Robin carefully sat on the cot, relieved when it didn't collapse, though it definitely groaned. "I'm going to go over the things for tomorrow."

Johan rolled his eyes, and Robin got up the courage to actually look up at him. Johan had pulled on a pair of jeans, but he was still bare-chested, and the temperature in the small room spiked at least ten degrees. A visual feast of golden skin, lean muscle but by no means muscle-bound, and a dusting of dark hair sent Robin's pulse racing. He turned away again, because lusting after his coworker was so damn wrong on so many levels.

Robin's brown curls—his mom called them shaggy—fell into his eyes, and he used them as cover to look a little more. Johan walked closer to the window, his belly at perfect eye level, a dark trail slipping into his pants, leading to… well, Robin's imagination could certainly fill in any gaps, and it did in spectacular fashion.

"Maybe I will go out," Robin said softly. Lord knew if Johan stayed in the room, especially like that, Robin wasn't going to be able to breathe. Robin grabbed his messenger bag and hurried to the door, almost forgetting his key, before leaving the room and hurrying down the hall to the stairs.

Outside on the cobbled street, Robin took a deep breath and slowly walked toward town. There was a small convenience-type store a few blocks away, and it would be good if he got some more water and a few snacks.

"Robbie."

Robin gritted his teeth and turned to find Johan striding toward him.

"You didn't have to leave the room so quickly." He fell into step with him.

"I'm Robin, not Robbie," he said firmly. He hated that nickname.

"Okay. You still didn't have to leave." Johan looked at him with his big, almost-mysterious brown eyes for long enough that Robin felt heat rising at the base of his spine. "Are you one of those prudish Americans who keeps himself covered all the time?"

"I'm not prudish," Robin said. "I just needed some fresh air and to get a few things." He continued on his way, doing his best to keep his attention on the way ahead and not on Johan's hotness.

"Do you not like guys? Is that it? You work for a gay tour company." Johan walked faster as Robin sped up. He hadn't meant to, but his legs just kept moving more quickly. "Maybe you're one of those people who doesn't like to be happy or something."

Robin came to an abrupt stop, opening his mouth to give Johan a tongue lashing, but he realized he was standing in front of the café where half his tour group sat, watching them. Well, they were watching Johan. No one ever paid that much attention to him.

Robin whirled on his heels and continued toward town. How dare Johan try to get into his head. "For your information, yes, I like guys, and I'm not a prude. Though you seem to have exhibitionist tendencies. Is what you've got really worth making sure everyone sees it?" He turned to Johan and cocked his eyebrow.

Johan smiled and didn't retort, which pissed Robin off a little more and actually raised his curiosity level. Damn it all to hell. Why was he doing this to himself? They had a job to do.

"Okay. So you're gay and not a prude. Got it." Johan continued walking behind him, and Robin did his best to ignore him. Maybe if he left the guy alone, he'd do the same for Robin. "But you are unhappy."

Robin stopped. Johan had to be the most un-German German he had ever met. As a rule, Germans tended to be somewhat reserved… well, they also tended to think that the German way was the best way to do everything, so maybe Johan was just too German for words. Robin wasn't sure, but he was pretty convinced that Johan was trying to drive him crazy.

"What makes you say that?" Robin paused just long enough to make the accusation and then turned away, seeing the store he wanted. They seemed about ready to close, so he ducked inside and got some water and a few snacks. Robin hoped Johan would go about his business, but Johan was waiting for him at the counter. Robin didn't remember him being this big of a pain. Of course, he also didn't remember him as anything other than a guy doing his best impression of the ape boy in a sideshow either.

Robin paid for his things and left the shop.

"You never smile."

"I do too," Robin countered while waiting for a car to pass. Then he purposefully headed back the way he'd come. At least he hoped it looked that way and not like he was trying like hell to run away.

"No, you don't," Johan said from farther behind him, but the tone, one Robin wasn't so sure about, made him pause. Johan closed the distance between them. "You smile when you think you're supposed to and when you don't want to cause the tourists distress, but you never really smile, not for yourself." He came even closer, sending heat racing through Robin, and Robin wondered if Johan was going to kiss him. They were certainly close enough. Johan's breath was fresh and smelled like minty sunshine. "You never smile with your eyes as well as your lips." His rumbling voice sent ripples through Robin. "You need to find what makes you happy."

"I'm happy. I like my life and what I do. I'm good at it and…." God, his protest sounded lame even to him. "I'm fine."

Johan nodded, and Robin turned back toward the hotel once again. He could feel Johan's gaze behind him every step of the way. At the café, he thought about stopping for a drink, but he needed to rest, so he waved and went to the hotel.

JOHAN HADN'T followed him all the way back. And Robin was tired. It had been a long day. The first day of a tour often was. After that, everyone usually fell into a routine and things became easier. God, he hoped so.

Robin used the bathroom, cleaned up, took his medications, and got into bed, the cot squeaking a little as he settled his weight. Robin hoped the damned thing didn't crash to the floor under him. He tried to find a comfortable position and finally settled on his side. Facing the wall didn't work, but lying on his other side was okay. He reminded himself that he only had two nights of this. He could muscle through.

Robin had just closed his eyes when the door to the hall opened, casting a slice of light through the room. He kept his eyes closed and tried to sleep. Johan was quiet, saying nothing as he used the bathroom and eventually climbed into bed. Robin cracked his eyes open as the lights turned out and got a flash of a perfect tight butt as Johan got under the covers. He bit his lower lip to stop the groan from knowing Johan was naked in the bed just a few feet away. Robin closed his eyes once again and tried to go to sleep. Somehow he managed to do it.

CHAPTER 2

ROBIN GROANED when he heard Johan getting out of bed. He cracked his eyes open and damned near got an eyeful as Johan closed the bathroom door. Robin knew he wasn't going to get any more sleep. Every time he'd moved all danged night, the cot had squeaked and groaned under him. He needed a shower, and when Johan came out of the bathroom in a pair of clingy boxers, Robin did his best not to ogle—he was a gay man, after all. He passed Johan with a *guten Morgen* before closing the door.

The facilities consisted of a handheld shower on the tub, so he shaved and took his pills, then climbed in and got himself washed as efficiently as possible. Once clean, he used one of the towels, wishing to hell his mind had been working. He should have brought his clothes in with him. Wrapping the towel around his waist, he opened the door and barreled right into Johan. The man was like a proverbial brick wall of muscle…

and heat. Robin managed to keep hold of his towel, stepped back, and hurried to his bag.

"What happened to you?" Johan asked in a tone Robin knew all too well and hated: pity.

"Lots of stuff," Robin said as he turned his back to Johan and dressed quickly. He wasn't pretty, and even his back had scars from all the procedures he'd had done over the years. Robin quickly pulled up his tan pants and shrugged on a white tour company polo shirt. Now that he was covered, he felt much better, not the center of attention. "Today we're staying in town, so you have the day off."

"I figured." Johan pulled on his shoes.

"You can come with us, if you'd like. Before we left, I made sure Albert included some money in the tour budget for entrance fees for you. I always do that for the drivers. Either that, or you can have the day on your own." Part of him wanted Johan to come along, but another part was nervous about spending the entire day with him.

Johan shrugged, which wasn't helpful in the least.

Robin grabbed his bag and left the room, heading downstairs to breakfast. He was the last one to show up, excluding Johan. The ladies were seated at one table and the guys at another, all of them talking softly. Robin growled under his breath and stepped right to the ladies table and sat. "Did you all sleep well?" he asked as though nothing were niggling at the back of his mind.

"Yes," Margaret answered, and the others nodded.

"Is something going on?" Robin asked as the young server offered him coffee. Robin declined in favor of orange juice, and she hurried away to get it for him. Lily shrugged, and the others suddenly found their plates extremely exciting. "Was something said?"

"No," Margaret answered, looking over at the guys. "Lily isn't comfortable around them, so we've been staying away, and…."

"Margaret, I'm fine," Lily said. "Really. Yesterday was hard for me, but I'm not afraid of men or anything. You don't have to shelter me."

Robin hoped this tension was just one of those things and that it would dissipate as the group got to know one another. He got some food from the breakfast bar, and when he returned, Johan had taken the seat across from him and had his big hands wrapped around a mug of coffee, breathing in the steam. Robin set down his plate and turned to the rest of the group. "We'll be leaving from in front of the hotel in about an hour. You have time to do a little shopping if you need to, and make sure you have on good walking shoes, because we'll be on our feet for a lot of the day."

Oliver groaned, but nothing else was said.

"Our guide will be from the local tourism board. She knows the town very well and can answer any questions you might have." Robin sat back down and began eating. The conversation in the room ramped up a little. Robin sighed and drank his juice.

"What are you doing today?" Johan asked.

"I'll be going on the tour, I suppose." Robin hadn't given it much thought. He didn't need to go. The guide was more than capable of taking the group through the town and then up to the Prince-Bishop's palace. She had done this tour at least six times for him alone.

"No." Johan put down his mug.

"Excuse me?" Robin raised his eyebrows.

"You heard me. The tourists are going with the guide this morning. Lunch is on their own, and then they'll visit the palace. So you get them started and turn them over to the guide, and I'll show you some real fun."

"And what if I wanted to go on the tour?" Robin pressed. He wasn't going to give in to whatever Johan wanted just because he snapped his fingers.

Johan rolled his eyes. "You could give the tour yourself after being on it… how many times? It has to be as boring as… well, you." The hint of a smile told Robin that Johan was teasing or else he'd have left the table and let the smartass sit there alone.

"Nice… really nice."

"Go see them off, and once they're gone, you're in my hands." Johan leaned forward and lowered his voice. "Completely." His eyes sparkled in the sunlight pouring through the windows, and Robin found himself nodding.

Why not? What was the worst thing that could happen? Well, if he thought about it too much, his imagination would run away with him.

"You need to have some fun."

"I see. And you've decided that you can help me with this." He was having too good a time sparring with Johan to stop. This alone was fun.

"Definitely." Johan finished his coffee and stood. "I think you need to see to the group. I am going to eat, and then when they are gone, we go."

Robin sighed. Johan was right—he had things he needed to do, and he could decide later if he was going to take Johan up on his offer.

ROBIN SAW the group off on their tour. They seemed excited, and he knew it was a good tour, with time for shopping, a stop at the market for snacks, lunch, and then the palace. He was a little disappointed because he always loved seeing the frescoed ceiling, but truthfully, he was interested in finding out what Johan had in mind.

Once the group was on their way, Robin went inside and up to the room, where Johan was waiting for him with a bag on the bed. "What's all this?"

"What we need for fun. Get your bathing suit and we go?" Johan said, and Robin shook his head.

He took a step back. "I don't have one…." He was about to say that he didn't go swimming.

Johan turned away and grabbed the bag. "I thought so. I have swim shorts for you. Come." He took Robin's hand and half tugged him out of the room, then locked the door. "Fun awaits."

Robin had his doubts about just what kind of fun this was going to be.

They walked to the tram station, and after Johan paid for their tickets, they got on.

"Where are you taking me?"

"To have some fun." He motioned to a seat and Robin sat down. "Nautiland."

Robin snickered. "What exactly is this Naughty Land?" He had pictures of sex dungeons racing through his head and figured he'd get off the tram at the next stop.

"It's a water park. There are slides, wave pools, bubble baths, and waterfalls." Johan grinned like a kid in a candy store.

Robin shied away, looking at Johan as though he'd lost his mind. "You have to be kidding." Robin slid onto the next seat to put some distance between them. "What are you trying to do? Scare half the population of Würzburg into thinking the Creature from the Black Lagoon has risen and taken up residence in their water park?" He shivered as he thought of all those people staring at him and his scars.

Johan shook his head. "No one is going to care. I saw them, remember? Did I run from the room screaming? No." He rolled his eyes. "I think the only one with an issue about how you look is you." Johan met his gaze with such intensity that Robin turned away. "You're all hung up."

"Fine." Robin crossed his arms over his chest.

"I brought a sun shirt for you anyway. You are really pale and will burn in the sun." Johan grinned at him, and Robin wanted to smack the man, but dang it, he was so cute.

"Then why did you let me go on?"

Johan shrugged. "You need to… how do you say? Vent? So I let you."

Robin rolled his eyes.

"Come. Our stop is next, and fun awaits!"

Johan jumped up like a kid as soon as the tram stopped. They got off and walked the block or so to the huge water park. Johan paid their entrance fees, refusing when Robin offered to pay his way. They each got a locker key and a wristband, and then they were inside. Robin wasn't surprised at the single locker room, and he changed into the shorts quickly, ignoring Johan and the old lady a row over as best he could. There were some things he never wanted to see, and there wasn't enough eye bleach in the world to blot out the sight of naked old lady.

Not that he was sexist or anything. He didn't want to see naked old man either.

Robin shrugged on the skintight swim shirt and turned to Johan, who wore a small square-cut suit that hugged his hips. Damn, he was stunning, and Robin wanted nothing more than to feast his eyes for a few minutes.

"You ready?"

"Are you sure they'll allow me to wear the shirt?"

"Yes. As long as it is a water shirt, they said it was okay." Johan closed his locker, and Robin did the same. Then he guided Robin into a huge pool room that echoed with cries of delight. "Come." Johan pointed upward. "Let's slide." He led the way to the ladder, and Robin followed.

"It's been a long time since I went swimming," Robin admitted.

"You not like the water?" Johan asked, pausing at the base of the steps, leaving room for others to pass.

"I do. It's…." Robin never liked how people stared at him, so he didn't go to the beach or public pools. Basically, for the last ten years or so, he'd avoided situations where he had to take his shirt off in public. "I didn't want to be seen, and my last boyfriend, well, I think he was more than happy not to have to see me… if you understand."

Johan narrowed his gaze, scowling. "Why were you with a man like that?" He started up the stairs, and as Robin pondered his question, he couldn't come up with a good answer. At least not one that didn't make him seem completely desperate and without any self-esteem at all.

At the top of the slide, Johan climbed on and slid through. Robin waited, and a group of kids went one after the other, laughing like crazy. Apparently there weren't a bunch of rules about waiting like in the US, so Robin took his turn, twisting and turning as he slid down and landed in a pool outdoors.

He popped up to a spray of water from the kids and Johan, who seemed to have put them up to it. Robin splashed back, and a water fight erupted that drenched all of them. God, it felt good to just let go, and when Johan lifted him off his feet, Robin sputtered as Johan tossed him into the water.

"That was mean," Robin challenged, doing his best to keep the grin off his face and failing miserably.

"Come on. Let's go again." They raced back inside and up the ladder, then went down again and again until Johan announced that the wave pool was starting. They hurried over and got in, riding the artificial waves and having an amazing time along with everyone else.

"Slide again?" Johan asked when the waves subsided, and they scurried over to climb the ladder again.

Robin completely lost track of time, though his belly eventually told him he needed to eat. He and Johan swam up to the snack bar area and got some food, then sat drip-drying on high stools.

"I love German fast food." Sausage and *pommes* out of a paper container, with curry ketchup. The stuff was to die for. "It beats a hot dog or McDonald's."

Johan nodded as he ate. "I love wurst and miss it when I travel. No one does sausage like us." He grinned and took a huge bite, setting down the rest of his sausage. After a few minutes, his gaze zeroed in on Robin with laser precision. "Were you in a car wreck?"

It took Robin a second to process what he was really being asked. "No. I was born with a bad heart. It didn't beat right. They did surgery when I was a baby to fix it. My heart was okay until I was a teenager, and then I had a heart attack and they had to take mine out and give me another. Then they found something wrong with one of my lungs, so I got a new one of those too, but not before they tried to fix mine." He figured he might as well explain everything. "I take pills every day to keep my body from rejecting the transplants, and so far it's working. But it means that my immune system is suppressed, so I have to be careful." Robin sighed. One reason he normally kept his scars hidden was so he didn't have to explain things like this to lots of people.

"You have many years of pain and recovery," Johan said with a slow nod of his head. "Why you do this? Guide tours. You could do lots of other things. You could stay home and be safer. Yes?"

"I like it, and I get to spend some time in Europe seeing things and being on my own." Robin finished his sausage and ate a fry dipped in curry ketchup. "I want more out of life than to sit home and be safe."

Johan continued nodding. "Then if you are here and like what you do, why are you not happy?"

That was the million-dollar question. "I guess because I was supposed to be here, leading tours with my boyfriend, and he dumped me for a man who was beautiful and perfect and… well, not me." The truth was, he felt like some unlovable creature, and Mason hadn't helped with that at all.

"He sounds like a big jerk," Johan said, and Robin had to agree.

"Mason and I never had sex with the lights on. Not once." Why in the hell he'd just said that was beyond him, least of all to Johan, but the words slipped past his lips before he could stop them. "Never. He told me when we broke up that he didn't want to see me, in case…." Robin held up a finger and then let it dangle limply. "I thought he loved me and wanted to be with me. Instead, I was some guy he took pity on. Turned out he'd been cheating on me for months before he broke up with me. The asshole," he added in a whisper.

"You are better off without him." Johan smiled as though he'd made some pronouncement of truth that was beyond dispute.

"I bent over backward for the jerk, and he…." For a long time, Robin had wondered what he'd done wrong and how he'd not made Mason happy. Robin hated how easily he could see now what Mason had been doing and how he'd taken advantage. It was so clear. The problem was, he was still in love with the asshole and wasn't sure how to get over him. That's what bothered Robin so damn much. It had been months—he should be able to let him go. "It isn't worth talking about." He ate his last bite, and Johan took care of the trash, then sat back down.

"There are saunas and a steam room if you want to do that," Johan offered.

Robin wasn't sure he was ready to be seen naked, so he hesitated.

"You do realize that we're going to the Friedrichsbad in Baden-Baden and you're going to have to get naked there."

Robin shook his head. "I see my tour groups to the door and then let them take the waters while I check on the rest of the itinerary and make phone calls." There, he had an answer that didn't sound like a complete cop-out.

Johan cocked his eyebrows and didn't say anything. Robin wondered if he was in for the guilting of a lifetime from him. "Then let's go and slide some more. I promised you a fun day, and if the sauna and steam rooms make you uncomfortable, then we can't have that." He stood and headed back toward the pools.

Robin couldn't help watching that butt of his swish slightly in that suit. Like the Pied Piper, he let Johan lead wherever he wanted them to go.

"THAT WAS an amazing time," Robin said as he and Johan got back on the tram toward the hotel around midafternoon. Robin figured the others should be finishing their tour of the Residence and he and Johan would be back in plenty of time.

"I got a message that we indeed have one more person joining the tour. He should be with us for dinner."

"Is that good?" Johan asked.

Robin shrugged. "Just another person, and it means maybe Albert won't be so cheap about some of the arrangements going forward." Robin continued staring at his phone as if he expected Albert to message him again at any second. He put the phone back in his pocket just as it buzzed. Robin rolled his eyes.

I emailed you the info.

Ok, Robin sent and put his phone away.

"See, you're smiling." Johan crowed a little, clearly satisfied with himself.

"Yes. I had a great time, and you made me happy. Does that make you feel better, oh wise one?" he teased, and Johan bumped his shoulder.

"Actually, it does." He sat back, smug as all hell for the rest of the ride on the beautifully sunny afternoon.

When they arrived at the hotel, the tour hadn't come back yet, so Johan took his bag up to the room and then they went to the café for a snack and something to drink. Within half an hour, the tourists straggled in, tired but with excited looks in their eyes.

"I had no idea something could be that beautiful," Kyle said as he sat next to Johan, with Billy sitting next to him.

"It's really stunning and very special for this part of the world," Grant said. "It's amazing the amount of work he produced and the amount of traveling he did." He took the seat next to Robin. "I saw some of his work in DC and it was stunning." In his excitement, he spoke faster by the second.

"Sweetheart," Billy said with a wave of his hand. "You don't have to know everything about everything." He turned to Kyle, and the two of them talked quietly.

Grant grew quiet as well, and Robin sighed. Yeah, Grant tended to be a bit of a know-it-all so far, but everyone needed a chance to become comfortable in the group.

"You all enjoyed the tour?" Robin asked a little loudly, cutting through the drama and trying to draw the rest of the tour group in.

"It was great," Lily said with what sounded like unforced excitement. The others echoed her sentiment, and Billy and Kyle melded into one of the ongoing conversations, while Grant seemed to do the same.

"Do you want coffee?" Johan asked him and Robin shook his head.

"Juice or water. I stay away from caffeine if at all possible," he explained, hoping Johan would understand.

"*Apfelschorle*," Johan said to the server, and Robin nodded. He loved the German concoction of fruit juice and seltzer. They often came in many fruit flavors and were refreshing and light, though the bottled ones were awful. Thankfully, they made their own here.

The server brought his drink, and Robin sipped it and sat still. He needed some time to rest a little. The pools had been so much fun, but it had required that he expend a lot of energy, and now his batteries were a little empty.

"Is it true that someone else is joining the tour?" Margaret asked from the next table.

"Yes. He'll be at dinner with us and can introduce himself." Robin sighed, and Johan leaned a little closer.

"Are you okay? You're really red…."

Robin nodded. "I just overdid it a little." He smiled because he didn't want Johan to feel bad. Today Robin had pushed the limits of what he could do. It was likely that after dinner, he'd go to bed and hopefully sleep the entire night… on that rickety damned cot. He finished his drink, which provided him with some energy, then paid the server and left the café, walking slowly back to the hotel.

One of the cobbles must have been loose. Robin didn't see it, but his foot went out from under him and he tumbled to the street. Thankful he hadn't hit his head and hopefully wasn't bleeding, he got to his knees.

"I have you," Johan said and gently helped him to his feet, then held his arm as he walked with him to the hotel.

"I'm okay." Robin kept taking inventory to make sure nothing was broken. The only thing injured was his pride, but he let Johan guide him inside and then up to their room, where Johan unlocked the door.

"Lie down, and I will get you a cloth."

Robin nodded and made his way around the bed to that damned cot.

"No." Johan hurried over, indicating the bed.

Robin sighed as he lay on the firm mattress, without a squeak to be heard. Johan placed a cool cloth on his forehead, and Robin closed his eyes. "I can't stay here. I have things I have to do." Robin tried sitting up after a few minutes, but Johan pressed him back down.

"I'll see to the group. You rest a little while." Johan pulled the curtains, and the room darkened. Then Robin heard him leave, closing the door softly behind him.

Robin kept his eyes closed and figured a little rest was what he needed. He'd taken his medications and all he needed was some sleep. He had overdone it a little, but didn't regret it. He'd had a ball, and every time they climbed to the platform with the slide, he'd gotten a view of Johan's backside that, well…. Robin knew what paradise looked like in a deep blue square-cut bathing suit. He smiled at the memory, and his headache spiked. He evened out his breathing, and the pain subsided. He really should take something, but he had to be careful with the other medications he was on. The best thing was to remain still and quiet, and the tension would pass. Taking off the cool cloth, he set it aside and soon drifted into a light sleep.

He woke with his headache gone and felt much better. The fatigue was a thing of the past… at least for now. Slowly he sat up and assessed his situation. There was no pain, his heart didn't seem to be racing, he wasn't warm any longer, and his head felt normal. Robin checked the clock. It was nearly time for dinner and to meet his addition to the tour group. He got to his feet, drank a cool glass of water, then headed downstairs.

The group hadn't returned yet, but he was sure they would once dinnertime approached. Robin wished he'd brought his laptop down with him. He needed to check the information on the person joining them, but he didn't want to go back up, so he went through the process of logging into the proprietary system through his phone. It was always a pain, but he was able to find the email.

"Hello, Robin."

A zing went up his spine, and he raised his gaze from his phone. He blinked, pushing away the momentary warmth that threatened to engulf him. "Mason, what are you doing here?" He glanced back at his phone and his heart sank. Mason was joining his group. Robin's stomach leapt as part of him wondered if Mason was here because he'd realized he wanted him back or if this was just a coincidence. Somehow he didn't think it was.

"I heard you were giving this tour, and I always wanted to visit this area… so I figured I'd see what you were up to." Mason smiled that completely disarmingly warm smile that Robin had fallen in love with years ago.

"You actually took this tour because I was leading it?" Robin asked, tamping down the touch of excitement. He reminded himself that Mason had left him, trampling his self-confidence under his feet as he did. "Do you really think that was a good idea?"

"We're friends, aren't we?" Mason asked, and Robin blinked, trying to figure out exactly what he was getting at.

"Is that what we are?" Robin asked. "After five years and plans to spend the rest of our lives together… now we're just friends?" He kept his voice even.

"Well, yeah. We were together for five years, but things didn't work out." Mason shrugged as though it were nothing. "It isn't a big deal… is it, Robin?" Mason leaned slightly closer.

Robin hated that smug, I-know-what's-best attitude. "You know what? It isn't a big deal, because you certainly aren't one," he retorted. "If you want to join the tour, go ahead. Have fun." Now it was Robin's turn to smile. "But if you cause any trouble, I have the right to leave you. Check the contract. And you'll see that I'm the one to determine if you're causing trouble." Robin stood. He needed some fresh air. "So be good."

"Is this really how it's going to be? It's been months since I've seen you, and I had some time off work, so I came over and thought I'd check on how you were doing." Mason sounded sincere, but Robin had his doubts.

"If you were so damn concerned about me, then you could have called and saved yourself all the expense and effort." He felt his backbone hardening. Still, Mason's eyes and the way his upper lip pressed outward just a touch were so familiar and comforting. He understood them.

"Robin, are you feeling better?" Johan asked as he came in. He took in Mason. "Are you the addition to the group?"

Mason visibly tensed. Not often was Mason second best in the looks department, but he certainly was to Johan, who was slightly taller, broader, and his features a little more chiseled than Mason's.

"Yes. Thank you. I am, Robin answered before turning slightly. "This is Mason. He's going to be joining us for the rest of the trip."

Johan looked at the two of them alternately as though trying to assess the tension. "Everyone is gathering for dinner." Johan motioned Mason forward. "The group is just through there."

Mason didn't argue, and Robin released the breath he'd been holding.

"That's my ex," Robin confessed, and Johan watched as Mason turned to join the others.

"We are ready for dinner," the young lady who had checked them in said, and Robin went on through, gathering the troops and getting them moving in the right direction.

"I need to check on the bus. I haven't done it today. I will be back in a few minutes." Johan flashed a quick smile and hurried off.

"Here is the extra key," the young lady said, handing Robin the key to Mason's room.

Robin slipped it in his pocket and went to dinner.

Robin liked the dining room. It had an old-fashioned, heavy, dark Germanic feel to it, as though it had been there for hundreds of years. It probably had been, for all he knew. Often buildings started out life with one purpose, were added on to, renovated, changed, and came through to modern times with a whole new lease on life. This could very well be one of those places. Robin took a seat at one of the empty tables, leaving a chair for Johan. The rest of the tour had turned quiet and seemed a little tired.

When most of the group was seated, Robin stood. "We have a new member to our group." He looked for Mason, surprised he wasn't already in the room. Mason came in, shaking his hands, and Robin realized he'd gone to wash up. "Everyone, this is Mason."

Everyone said hello, and Billy and Kyle, who came in right behind Mason, walked to where Robin was sitting and took the seats across from him.

"How was your day, guys?"

"Pretty awesome," Billy said. "I'm not really into all the architecture and art stuff, but it was super cool and I learned a lot."

Kyle nodded. "I took an art class in college, and it was really cool to see one of the pieces the professor talked about in real life. I loved just walking through the cathedral. My mom would have loved it and been totally blown away. It was so big."

"And it's eight hundred years old," Mason said as he pulled out the chair next to Robin and sat. "I'm Mason."

"This is Kyle and Billy," Robin supplied, and looked toward the dining room door, suppressing a growl.

"I think Robin was saving that seat," Kyle said, bless his heart.

"For me, I'm sure. Robin and I are… old friends." Mason flashed his smile, but Kyle didn't seem to be buying Mason's explanation. Robin didn't want to make waves at dinner, so he kept quiet and watched as the servers brought out trays of plates.

Johan came in and joined one of the other tables, and Robin turned back to his group, figuring he might as well make the most of it.

"I'm glad you enjoyed yourself. Tomorrow is totally different. Baden-Baden is an amazing town with upscale shopping."

"What does Baden mean?" Kyle asked.

"It's a spa town—has been since the Romans. There are ruins there that we'll be able to see. But our first stop will be the Friedrichsbad. It's our spa stop."

"Are you sure?" Mason asked, turning to him with his I-know-best look that made Robin want to smack him. "It's the more traditional of the spas."

Robin flashed Mason a warning look, which he seemed intent on ignoring. "It's what was advertised on the tour." Robin didn't change anything that had been billed with the package. If tour members didn't wish to go, that was their decision, but he wasn't going to upset people by removing something they had paid for. "It will be fine."

"So you're going," Mason said, the challenge in his voice as clear as a bell.

"You are going with us, aren't you?" Kyle asked.

"I will have some things to do, and I usually get them done while you enjoy the spa. That way everything can be ready when you're done." There. That sounded completely reasonable and not at all like he was scared half to death at the thought of being naked, his scars on display in front of everyone.

Robin turned his attention to his plate of bratwurst, fried potatoes, and green beans. It smelled heavenly, and he hoped he could figure out a way to change the subject. Thankfully Mason and Kyle started talking about football. Robin tried to think of something to speak with Billy about, but he seemed more intent on watching Kyle, the same way Robin found his gaze traveling to Johan in each spare moment.

"Are you listening?" Mason asked, and Robin pulled his attention away from Johan. "I was saying that some of the guys may want to go to the Caracalla Therme instead, and—"

Robin side-kicked Mason under the table, and he startled. "Everyone is welcome to do what they're comfortable with. But the tour already includes the one bath, and the arrangements are made and paid for." That should shut Mason up. Mason was a jerk, always needing to be the center of attention. "After the spa, which is amazing—"

"So you're going," Mason pressed, and Robin ground his teeth and thought about kicking him again, but it wasn't going to do any good. Mason's smug smile told him all he needed to know.

"I can go." The things he did to keep the peace.

"Then we'll go together," Mason said with a satisfied grin as Robin tried to figure out what his game really was.

"Actually, I'm going as well," Johan piped up from behind him. "Robin and I already arranged to spend the day together." Johan winked as Robin turned to him.

Both Kyle and Billy snickered, and Mason's lower jaw just about hit the table.

"Everything okay?" Robin asked quietly, and Johan shrugged. *Damn.* Robin realized he'd been rescued once again. Johan had probably just come over because he'd overheard what was said.

"Everything is fine. The bus is good, and we'll be ready first thing in the morning. What time did you want everyone gathered?"

"I was going to tell them eight." Robin's nervousness slipped away and he felt in control once again.

"The bus will be ready," Johan said, then went back to his seat.

Robin did his best to ignore Mason and finish his dinner. Billy and Kyle were talking with Mason, and Robin used the distraction to eat quickly before excusing himself. He went outside into the early twilight, looking out toward the river and bridge. He wanted to call Albert and give him a piece of his mind, but then how could Albert have known this was his ex?

Robin clenched his fists and turned back to the hotel. God, why did Mason have to show up? This sucked big-time. He had to be nice to him and treat him like any other member of the group. It was so damned frustrating and so not fair.

Robin clamped his eyes closed when he heard footsteps approach. A familiar touch rested on his shoulder, and he tensed. "What do you want, Mason?"

"Hey. I didn't mean to get in the middle of things with you and the driver." Mason stood next to him. Robin could feel it, but he kept his eyes closed. He didn't want to see Mason's big brown eyes or the way he made himself look innocent and gentle. That was an act. Robin knew that now, and he'd endured it during the rip-the-Band-Aid-off breakup.

"Johan… he and I work together, and he's a nice guy." Robin might have fantasized about him a few times, especially that afternoon in that bathing suit, but he had no illusions that a guy like Johan was going to be interested in him. He'd learned his lesson with the man standing next to him.

"So, you aren't dating him?" Mason asked, and Robin shook his head. "Then you wouldn't mind if I talked to him."

Robin opened his eyes and turned to Mason. "No, go right ahead." He smiled and shook his head as it faded quickly. "God, I was in love with you, and I spent the last six months wondering what I could have done to make you happy." He stepped into Mason's space. "You pulled the damn rug out from under me, and I fucking let you." He shook with anger and hurt as the words came pouring out of him. "Now you show up and want to act as if nothing happened and everything is just fine and hunky-dory between us. We're friends now, pals." Robin vibrated as he tried to contain his rage. "Well, friends don't treat people the way you treated me, and they certainly don't undermine me in front of the rest of the tour group. So if you want to be part of the tour, that's great, but step out of line…."

He leaned closer. “So help me, I’ll rip your little walnuts off.”

Mason stepped back. “What happened to you?” He had the audacity to look shocked.

“I don’t know. You dumped me two days before Christmas at my parents’ house. In front of my entire family.” Robin wanted to tear his head off at the moment. “Then you left, you fucking left, at Christmas. I wanted to crawl into a hole, and let’s not go into the things you said.” He glared at Mason, hard.

“Things weren’t working for us. You have to know that.”

“Oh, quit with that crap. You had plenty of time to decide what you wanted. You knew, and you decided to wait until you and I disagreed about something, and then—*wham*—you hit me with everything and left. Don’t you dare waltz in here and play this ‘we’re old friends’ shit.” Robin curled his lips upward. “There’s a thin line between love and hate, and honey, you walked over that line the minute you sat down at that table. So tread lightly.” Robin turned away. He was through with this for now.

He went back inside to find the dining room was emptying out. Robin got a glass of water and sat at one of the few occupied tables.

“Are we really going to a spa tomorrow where everyone is naked?” Oliver asked.

“Yes. It’s very natural here. There will be men and women, old and young. It doesn’t matter, because after a few minutes in the saunas and steam rooms, you’re going to be so relaxed, you aren’t going to care. Trust me.” Robin looked up to see Javier patting Oliver’s hand. It was the nicest gesture of comfort or even caring he’d seen between them.

"Really?" Oliver colored deeply. "Who is going to want to see this old body anyway?" he groused softly.

"This isn't about being seen, but relaxing and getting cleaner than you have ever been in your life. There's no real sexiness about it. Just let it go and don't worry about it. That's what I did the last time I was there." And that had been one of the hardest things Robin had ever done in his life. He hadn't been there with a tour group, so it didn't really matter who saw him. Tomorrow was a different situation, but he'd already let Mason goad him into going, and he wasn't going to back out.

"Okay." Oliver finished his coffee and got up from the table. Javier followed, and they left the dining room.

Robin figured it was time for him to go up to his room. Most of the group seemed to have headed out to the cafés for dessert, but he was exhausted, and he'd have to be up early so he could be ready when everyone else needed to go. He certainly wasn't looking forward to another night on that damned cot. But it was one last night, and then hopefully something would change.

ROBIN GENTLY climbed onto the cot in the now-dark room. He was as tired as he could ever remember being. The confrontation with Mason had taken the last of his energy, and once the river of pain and anger had stopped flowing, he'd been wrung out. Johan would be to bed eventually, but Robin needed to rest now.

The evening was warm, and even with the window open, the air didn't move. Robin tried to get comfortable but couldn't find a good position, though he finally fell asleep out of pure exhaustion.

"Hey," Johan whispered in his ear, and Robin slid his eyes open. "You're tossing and turning, and that damned cot squeaks all the time." Johan tugged him off the cot. "Come on. You need rest, and I need to sleep if I'm going to be able to drive the bus in the morning." Johan guided him to the bed and pulled back the covers. Robin was too tired and muddleheaded to give it much thought. He slid beneath the covers and closed his eyes, barely able to stay awake.

At some point in the night, Robin must have shifted, and he woke warm, almost hot, pressed to Johan as though his life depended on it.

Johan slept on, his breathing regular, breath sliding over Robin's ear, and Robin was as excited as he'd ever been. And if Johan's hand were any lower, he'd be well aware of just how excited Robin was. Carefully, Robin slipped out of Johan's arms and climbed off the bed. As quietly as he could, he went to the bathroom, used the facilities, and then took his morning pills. He needed to get moving. There would be a light breakfast available in half an hour, and the bus left at eight.

Johan was awake when Robin came out, sitting on the edge of the bed in a pair of sleep shorts and nothing else, a sight to behold.

"Did you sleep well?"

"Until you got out of bed," Johan answered, wiping his hands down over his face.

"It's almost seven. I have to get downstairs and get this tour day started, and you need to make sure the bus is ready and…." Robin set his suitcase on the bed and pulled out clothes for the day.

He felt more than heard Johan come up behind him, his big, strong hands sliding down his shoulders and arms, stilling him. Then, with gentle force, he tugged Robin back, pressing him to his chest. "Just relax. Everything is going to be fine."

Robin tensed. He didn't want to move and break the contact, but it made him nervous too. Okay, definitely more excited than actually nervous.

Johan slid his hands around Robin's chest and belly, holding him tighter, resting his head next to Robin's, just standing still and quiet in the fresh morning air.

"But I have to get going," Robin argued with no heat whatsoever. This was too nice to want it to stop.

"So do I," Johan agreed, also without moving. "Just relax. Everything is going to be fine today." Johan held him a little tighter before releasing his arms. Robin hoped his knees didn't buckle from under him, and he managed to stay on his feet. If something as simple as being held made him light headed, he was in trouble.

Robin slowly reached for his clothes and dressed once Johan's hotness was safely behind the bathroom door. Time to get his day started, even if Robin's mind lingered on the night before. Johan was still bathing when Robin left the room with his suitcase. Downstairs, he put his luggage with the others and headed to breakfast.

It was readily apparent that some of the guys had been out late and probably drank a little too much. Kyle seemed okay, but Billy sat at the table with his head in his hands, groaning softly to himself.

"Drink this," Kyle said, setting a glass filled with tomato juice in front of him. "You need something in your belly, and this will help clear your head. It's like a Bloody Mary without the alcohol."

Robin wondered what was in it as he sat down.

After a few drinks, Billy seemed somewhat revived, fanning his face. "What the hell did you put in there?"

"Hot sauce," Kyle told him. "The cure for what ails you. Now drink the rest of it."

Billy set the glass down, drank a full glass of water, and then got some more tomato juice to cut down his drink. At the very least he seemed to be thinking more clearly.

Robin ate a roll with some butter and some cheese, keeping it light, as others wandered in and sat down. "I hope everyone had a great evening last night." Robin stood at his place. "Johan will bring the bus around a little before eight. Just bring him your bags, and he'll load them in the bus, and then we can get going. The drive to Baden-Baden is about three hours or so. It's a beautiful town, with grand buildings, a stunning shopping plaza, and even Roman ruins. We will be heading into the baths at eleven, and we need to be on time. You don't need to bring anything with you other than fresh clothes to change into when you're done."

A couple hands went up. "Why?" Grant asked. "I just put these on."

"Because once you've been through the spa, you will feel cleaner than you've ever felt in your life, and putting on clothes you've already worn is going to feel awful. Trust me. They have an entire regimen for you to follow, and it will take two to two and a half hours that will fly by. So finish your breakfast and join us on the bus at seven forty-five." Robin sat back down to finish his breakfast.

Johan sat down beside him with a plate, eating quickly.

"Isn't this nice," Mason said as he sat down at the end of the table. Robin turned to glare at him, but Mason seemed intent on his plate. Still, Robin had noticed the disapproval in his voice, as though Mason had anything to say about who he ate with.

"We're going to get our stuff," Kyle said, full of energy and half carrying a still-hungover Billy along with him.

Johan finished his coffee in a last few gulps. "I'm going to get the bus brought around." He left, and Robin once again found himself alone, or relatively so, with Mason.

Part of him did a little flush of excitement, out of a sort of muscle memory. Things between the two of them had been heady and exciting when they'd first met. Robin hadn't thought that someone hot, like Mason, would be interested in him, and it had really seemed as though Mason didn't care about his physical limits. They dated and had fun together. They didn't make love right away, but waited, and Robin fell hard for Mason's patience and gentleness.

"Did you sleep okay?" Robin asked, trying to say anything to alleviate the awkwardness, and finding it hard. They had been together for five years.... Small talk seemed stupid with someone you knew really well—or thought you did.

"Yes. It was a fun last night. I went out with the guys, and we found a place to dance." Mason met his gaze. "I didn't have to worry about getting tired or moving too fast. I could dance and go to my heart's content. It was really fun." Mason ripped a bite off his roll and shoved it into his mouth.

"You never did like to wait for anyone." Robin had always brought up the rear with Mason. He had his own speed.

Mason tore off another bite. "It's nice sometimes not to have to. And I didn't have to be in at any particular time. The club we found closed at two, and we danced and I met some guys. They were fun, and we…."

Robin shook his head, and Mason finally seemed to get that Robin wasn't interested in his exploits. "I'm glad you had a good time." He pushed the chair back. "I'll see you on the bus." He needed to get the hell away before his hurt took over. Robin was well aware that Mason's comments were directed at him. He'd thought that Mason understood that he had limits. But any empathy turned out to be a sham, just like a lot of the things Robin thought Mason had accepted. Maybe Robin wasn't worth being with at all and should just accept that he was going to be alone.

Robin went outside, standing in front of the hotel to get a little air. Johan pulled up in the bus, then stepped off, smiling, and Robin forgot about the crap with Mason for a few seconds.

"Are they about ready?" He stepped closer, looking around. "Where is everyone?"

"Getting their things," Robin answered, his heart beating a little faster as Johan stood still, locking Robin in his heated gaze.

"Did you sleep better last night?" Johan whispered, and Robin nodded, his mouth going dry. He was about to answer when Oliver and Javier came out, with Javier pulling their luggage. Robin stepped away and collected their room keys as Johan got busy loading their luggage.

"Take your seats, and we'll get going as soon as everyone is on the bus."

Lily and Margaret came out, as did a few of the other couples. Grant shuffled his feet, still half asleep as he handed over his luggage and keys, then schlepped onto the bus. Billy and Kyle appeared as well, with Billy looking marginally better.

"You can probably sleep a little on the bus if you like," Robin offered to Billy, who smiled slightly, dragging after his late night.

Couple by couple, they climbed onto the bus. Robin made sure he had all the room keys and turned them in at the desk and made sure the billing was correct before leaving and getting on the bus. Most everyone was quiet, with Oliver and Javier being the exception. They seemed to be having some sort of quiet fight, with plenty of glaring and hissing under their breath.

"We're all set," Robin said, and Johan pulled away.

Much of the ride occurred in silence, which Robin was grateful for. Mason sat toward the back of the bus, and Robin up near Johan, slumped in his seat, replaying the events of the night before in his mind. It had been so amazing waking up in Johan's arms. But what was he going to do going forward? Robin shifted in his seat, watching the back of Johan's head.

Robin tensed as Mason sat down next to him, pulling Robin out of his Johan-watching haze. "I see you watching him."

"Is that really any of your business?" Robin asked in a whisper. "You made your feelings clear several months ago, and now you… what?"

Mason turned, looking as though he was about to go back to his seat, but he shrugged instead. "You know the facts of your condition as well as anyone. You had a heart transplant a little over six years ago, and that means…."

Robin glared at Mason. He was well aware of exactly what that meant. Heart transplant patients were lucky if they lived ten, twelve years after the transplant. That fate echoed in his mind sometimes, like a ticking clock winding down. He used to imagine that his new heart only had so many beats for him, and once they were gone….

"Yes. To you that means I shouldn't be happy." Robin turned away. "Just go back to your seat and leave me alone." He looked out the window as they traveled through the countryside. And eventually Mason returned to his seat.

Robin had always suspected that was part of the reason Mason had left. Every year that passed was one year closer to when Robin's borrowed heart ran out. Robin had always known that was going to be difficult for anyone in his life. Robin had wasted five of his precious years on Mason. Maybe it was too much to expect anyone to be truly interested in him once they knew how little time he had left. Still, Robin was determined to make the most of what he had. But love, happily ever after, all of that fairy-tale stuff, maybe that was too much for him to hope for from anyone.

BADEN-BADEN WAS just as quaint and beautiful as Robin remembered. Johan parked near the spa, and Robin got lockers for everyone. He was still hesitant about going in, but Johan smiled at him and handed the attendant their tickets, then gently ushered him into the changing area.

"You have nothing to be afraid of," Johan said, though his words didn't settle Robin's rattled nerves. "You've been through a lot, and if anyone can't see the courage it took, then they are not worth anything." Johan opened his locker and started stripping off his clothes.

The room was otherwise empty; the rest of the guys had evidently moved on. At least that was what

Robin thought, until Mason ambled in, catching first his eye and then Johan's. He actually leered as Johan pulled off his shirt. Robin wanted to smack him, hard, but turned away and slowly disrobed.

With each piece of clothing he removed, Robin became more and more self-conscious. He closed his eyes and dropped his pants. It wasn't because of Johan and Mason—they had seen him before. He was worried about the people in the steam rooms and saunas. Finally, he pushed down his underwear and set all his dirty clothes in the locker, along with his small bag of clean clothes and shoes, and closed the door, locked it, and headed for the showers without looking to either side.

"Keep your head held high," Johan said as he came up behind him. "You have nothing to be ashamed of."

Robin wasn't so sure, but when he turned, Johan stared at him—or specifically, Johan was looking at his ass with heat. It sent a ripple of excitement running through Robin that lasted until he stepped under one of the showerheads and turned it on, sending a deluge of water rushing over him. It felt more like being under a waterfall than a shower. Robin washed, and Johan did the same.

Mason came in at some point, and Robin did his best to ignore him. When he was done, he picked up a towel and headed to the warm sauna, as directed by the attendant.

The wooden room, filled with lounges, was still. All the guys were lying with towels partially covering them. Robin nodded to a few who acknowledged him. It seemed the best thing in an environment like this was to keep to himself. In this case, privacy was just keeping his eyes to home. He lay down on his towel, leaving one empty lounge next to him, which Johan settled on.

For once, Billy, Kyle, Grant, Oliver, and Javier were quiet. There was no chatter at all, just complete silence. Robin closed his eyes and let his thoughts drift a little. Of course they floated right to the man next to him. That lasted until Mason came in, and he insisted on talking.

"Mason," Johan said as soon as he sat down. "This is quiet time. Speak softly if you must, but preferably not at all." He lay back down, and Robin smiled and snickered, rolling his head to face Johan. He was truly as beautiful as any of Robin's imaginings. His chest was perfection and filled with each breath, his legs long and flawless. Robin turned away and glanced down at himself, then closed his eyes. It would be best if he just concentrated on himself and forgot about everyone else.

After ten minutes, Robin moved to the hot sauna, sitting and sweating for a few minutes before moving on. The extreme heat put a strain on his body, so after another shower, he hit the warm steam room and sat in there, relaxing, before skipping the hot steam and heading for another shower and the mineral bath.

He rested on the side of the pool with the other guys, who talked softly. Mason came in, followed by Johan, who hung up his towel and lowered himself in the water. All the other guys did their best not to look like they were looking, but they failed. Everyone single one of them took in Johan's masculine beauty. It was damned near impossible not to.

"That was quite a show," Robin teased in a soft whisper as Johan stood next to him.

Johan shrugged without looking away, keeping his attention on Robin. Clearly he didn't care what anyone else thought.

Robin lowered himself so only his neck was above the water and let the extra softness and warmth caress him like a gentle, perfect blanket on a cool day. He closed his eyes and just relaxed, ignoring everything around him. The others came and went, heading to the bubbly pool and finally the round exercise pool under the massive Victorian dome. Robin had seen it, but this felt amazing to him, so he stayed where he was until his skin pruned. Then he went back to the locker room, skipping the soap massage, showered for the last time, and went to the meditation room, where an attendant helped wrap him in a bath sheet. He lay on a cot in the dim room, dozing for half an hour. Then he dressed and half oozed out of the spa to sit on a nearby bench with a bottled water, waiting for the others.

"I was wondering what happened to you," Oliver said when he and Javier emerged a little while later. Robin wasn't sure how to take that comment, his mind going instantly to his scars. "You didn't follow the rest of us." Oliver sat down on the bench next to him.

"I'm going to get a beer." Javier pointed to a nearby park and trotted off.

"Are you enjoying things on your trip?" Robin asked, pleased that his scars weren't the topic of the day.

"Yes," Oliver answered halfheartedly. "Between you and me, I think I feel like a fool." He turned toward where Javier had gone. "I thought that this trip would be fun and that he and I would get closer. But I…." Oliver sat back. "I'm way too old for him, and I know it. I tried dressing younger and even did the things he liked…."

"But you can't keep up?" Robin asked.

"Yeah. He has so much energy, and I'm over fifty. My spirit wants to be young, but my body hates me.

So…." Oliver turned back to the imposing spa building. "I'm supposed to be tweeting interesting things about my trip so Javier and his friends can be amused and retweet them. I don't get the whole Twitter thing. I really don't. Life in 280 characters doesn't interest me. Maybe if I was younger, I'd get it, but I don't." He sighed. "And I don't think I want to. Let the young go for it." Oliver shrugged. "I don't know what to do."

Robin always hesitated to give advice to anyone on his tour groups. It was a surefire way to have everything blow up in one's face. "What do you want to do?" He looked at Oliver, meeting his gaze. "Maybe decide what you want, not what you think he wants, and talk to him." There. That was as close to actual advice as he was willing to come. Yeah, it was platitudes, but it seemed fairly safe. "Oh, and go get a beer." He smiled, and Oliver did the same, then headed the same way Javier had gone.

"You look comfortable," Mason said as he approached once Oliver had left.

Robin groaned and closed his eyes. Maybe if he ignored him, Mason would simply go on his way and leave him alone for a little while. "I am." He stretched out to make the bench seem as uninviting as possible.

"I was wondering if you wanted to get something to eat?" Mason sat on the edge of the bench anyway. "That was really fabulous. I feel more relaxed and clean than I ever have been in my life. And that building, what a place. That dome under the pool was stunning. I lay in the water just looking up at it."

Robin turned. "Mason, for God's sake, stop talking. Have you ever noticed that when you want to say something but don't have the guts to, you run on and on about nothing at all? Quit prattling and either say what you want to say or just go get yourself a beer and something to eat." His patience with Mason was already running thin, and the relaxation hangover from the spa was quickly wearing off.

"Okay. I see why you're drawn to Johan. The man is gorgeous. None of the guys could take their eyes off him. Hell, as soon as he stepped into the mineral bath, the air warmed by ten degrees. The guy is smoking hot." Thankfully Mason kept his voice down, though he hadn't said anything that wasn't true.

"And your point is?"

"I see the way you look at him, and you two shared a room. It's so easy for you to think there's something more there than there actually is. A guy like that, he isn't going to go for someone like you… or me." The last part sounded extremely tacked on, probably so he didn't sound like an ass, but he was already too late. "I'm telling you this as a friend."

"You know something? Johan is my driver, and he's been nice to me." Robin shifted on the bench so he could look Mason square in the eye. "You know what he said to me when he saw my scars? He said I should hold my head high because those scars said that I had more courage than anyone he'd ever known." Robin swallowed hard, pushing forward. "And he's right. You've never been through what I have, and hopefully you never will have to. I went through hell, and when I came out the other side, I got a new lease on life. Granted, it's only a temporary reprieve. The heart they implanted will wear out faster than a normal heart would, and hopefully because of advances in care and medications, the heart will last longer than the ten or twelve years they expect." He collected his thoughts a second. "Not that I'm saying that anything is going on between

Johan and me, but….” He might have wanted there to be something, but he didn't live his life with his head in the clouds. He'd be more than happy to have Johan as a friend. “But the hardest thing about only having maybe twelve years or so is that I spent nearly half of them with someone like you.” Robin stood and took a few steps toward the beer garden. “I thought you loved me, Mason. I don't know if you ever did or not. Maybe you were only with me out of pity.”

“I did love you,” Mason said softly.

“But not enough to stay, and now that I'm happy, and sure—” Robin shook his head slowly. “—there's the possibility that I like someone else… you're jealous. Well, that boat has sailed, and you need to get over yourself. You made your decision, and that's it.”

Whatever reaction Robin expected, it wasn't the laughter he received. “I'm not jealous. You and I had some good times, but I don't think you're the guy for me. Just like I don't think I'm the one for you.”

“So, what is all this? Why book yourself on my tour and act like you're my overbearing big brother… like I'm not capable of making my own decisions?” He hardened his expression and waited for an answer he was determined to get.

“I came on this tour because I wanted to see Germany. And I know you. You're a good tour guide, and I thought it would be fun.” Mason put his hands in the air. “Look, I'm sorry for the way I broke up with you, and I'm sorry for a lot of things. But I couldn't get over… certain things.” He turned away. “And you needed to move on with your life, just like I did. But that doesn't mean that I hate you or wish you ill. You're a good man, and you deserve someone who will make you happy.”

"Even if I only have a few years to live?" Robin pressed, glancing up to the spa when he saw movement at the top of the steps. "How about you let me worry about my life and you figure out yours? And as for this friendship you're so interested in having, why don't you let me see what kind of friend you can be? Now, I suggest you go get something to drink and some lunch. I have work to do." It was a brush-off, but he needed some time away from Mason for the moment. Thankfully, Mason heaved himself up and headed off toward the beer garden.

"Ladies, how was it?" Robin asked as the four of them came down the steps.

"Liberating," Lily said with a grin that seemed completely genuine. "I never would have done this while I was with my husband, and it was glorious. I feel like a new woman." She swung an arm around Margaret's neck. The others nodded.

"Awesome." Robin turned. "Some of the others have headed to the beer garden in the park." He pointed the way. "There are also restaurants in town. But get something to drink. Did any of you take the waters inside?" When they all nodded, he said, "Okay. The water in the spa is slightly radioactive. So I hope you didn't drink too much, or you won't need a night-light."

Thankfully they all chuckled at his joke.

"We're going to head to town. There was a restaurant I read about in one of the guidebooks that we wanted to try," Margaret supplied, and the four ladies headed off.

"The bus leaves at three," Robin reminded them, and thought about what he wanted for lunch. Damn, it was good to see Lily walking with a lightness in her step, after just a few days. Maybe this tour was what each of them needed.

Robin directed Billy and Kyle, along with Grant, to the beer garden when they emerged.

"Are we going to be able to see the Roman ruins?" Grant asked earnestly. The other two rolled their eyes. "Come on, guys. How often do you get to see something that's two thousand years old?"

"He's right. We can go after lunch," Billy said, looking much better and less hungover, watching Kyle closely. "We can get some lunch—no beer, please—and then go."

Robin gave them directions, and they headed off along with the others as they came out. Johan was the last to exit the spa, and he walked right up to Robin.

"Why did you leave so quickly?" Johan asked, taking Robin's bag of clothes.

"The hot sauna and steam rooms put too much strain on me, and I had to be careful because the water is radioactive. I didn't drink any, and I cut my visit a little short." There were many things he needed to be careful of, but he'd gotten used to it.

"Then you need something to drink and some lunch." Johan took his hand and laced their fingers.

Robin checked his watch. "Where are we going?" he asked as Johan steered them away from the beer garden.

"I know a place," Johan said with a grin, leading him away from the center of town, down a quiet, mostly residential street to a small local restaurant. They went inside, and Johan was greeted by the bartender, as well as the patrons. "This is home," Johan explained as they slid into chairs at a table in the corner. He called out in German, and soon a huge Schorle and a beer were brought to the table.

"Where's the menu?" Robin responded, in German as well. It seemed this wasn't a place tourists came. Robin was among the real people of Baden-Baden.

"Fritz is making us something special," Johan explained in German, and Robin nodded. Because of the tours he led, most of his life was spoken in English. It was nice to be immersed in German culture and camaraderie for a while. "He's my brother. This is my family's restaurant."

A huge, muscular man emerged from the kitchen in chef's whites, and Johan stood to greet his brother. The German was rapid-fire, and Robin had a little trouble keeping up, but he got the gist of what they were saying.

"He's good at what he does," Robin said, coming to Johan's defense.

"This is Robin," Johan said with a smile.

Fritz stared at him in what Robin could only decipher as disbelief. They shook hands, and Fritz turned back to Johan, motioning for them to sit back down. Then he turned and went back to the kitchen. Robin wondered just what had transpired, but he found out ten minutes later when three women rushed in, sliding them both over in the wooden booth seating.

The conversation flew quickly in the local dialect, which Robin didn't catch all of. The words were familiar, but the usage was so different.

"Mother, Marta, Louisa, this is Robin. He's the tour guide." Johan grinned a little nervously. "He speaks German but not Alemannic." Johan introduced each of them, and Robin wished he could stand to greet them, but he was hemmed in already.

"May we speak English?" Marta asked. "I'd like to practice. I'm hoping to attend university in America, and I want to better my English." She had a kind, lilty voice with a sweet face and bright eyes.

"Of course." Robin smiled, and she returned it. "So what stories can you tell me about Johan?" he asked.

His mother's eyes widened, Louisa snickered, and Marta laughed outright.

"I like him. I think he will keep up with you," Marta said, turning to Johan.

That was the one thing Robin wasn't so sure about. Like Oliver, Robin wasn't going to be able to keep up with anyone for very long. "I'll try."

Johan checked his watch as his mother got up and returned with plates as Fritz emerged from the kitchen with platters of food that he placed in the center of the table before sitting at the end. Apparently this was an impromptu family dinner, and Robin was invited.

"How long you know my son?" Johan's mother asked.

"We've worked together on and off for a few months," Robin answered. "He's been very good to me."

She nodded. "I hope so. I raise him right." She fussed a little over Johan, filling his plate with sausage, spätzle, and vegetables. Everything smelled amazing, and before he could say anything, Mrs. Krause had filled him a plate too. "He never brings people home to us." She seemed pleased as punch about it, which surprised Robin.

"We've known for quite a while that Johan prefers men," Louisa said. "He has never brought anyone for us to meet." They all seemed as interested in him as anything. "Where you grow up?" she asked before he could take a bite. His stomach rumbled at the scent of onions, bacon, and spices from the sausage that came off his plate.

"My family is from Milwaukee. We have a tavern there that also serves food. Much like this one. Mama serves bratwurst and sauerkraut. She's famous for it in the neighborhood. And good, German beer. Dad serves a few quality small, German-style American beers as well. But none of the big mass-produced stuff. People can get that anywhere." Robin finally took a bite, rolling his eyes.

"Does your mother make spätzle?" Mrs. Krause asked.

"Yes, but not as good as this," Robin said as he continued eating between the questioning. Mrs. Krause grinned, and Robin knew he'd said the right thing. Robin had to be careful with all the butter and richness in the food, but the vegetables were amazing, with plenty of flavor, and the sausage was spicy and surprisingly lean. Before his plate emptied, Mrs. Krause was already getting ready to fill it.

Johan said something quietly to his mother—Robin wasn't sure what—and she set the spoon down. Robin was grateful. He did ask for a little more of the vegetables, though.

"Marta said she is getting ready for university. Do you work here in the restaurant?" Robin asked Louisa.

"Sometimes when I'm needed."

"Louisa is bank manager," Mrs. Krause said very proudly.

Johan turned to him. "Louisa is a rising star with one of the banks here. She was always very good with numbers. Marta is going to be a doctor, I think… for animals."

"Ah. A veterinarian. How wonderful. Are you going to care for small animals or larger ones?" Robin asked. "I think it would be cool to be able to care for horses."

"I haven't decided," she answered. "I'd like to care for all animals and work in a zoological garden."

"Marta was always fascinated with lions and tigers," Johan explained further, and Robin finished his vegetables, belly about ready to burst. He sipped his Schorle and listened as family conversation swirled around him.

"Dessert?" Mrs. Krause asked.

Johan glanced at his watch. "Robin and I have to get back to town and meet the tour." He stood, kissed his mother on the cheek, and hugged both of his sisters and his brother.

Robin slid out of the booth as well and shook hands with all four of them, paying plenty of compliments. "Thank you for everything. The meal was amazing. It was a pleasure to meet you all." Robin waited as Johan said goodbye to his family, and they headed out. "You didn't tell me we were going to meet your entire family." He hoped he didn't look like a schlub to them.

"You were fine. They all liked you." Johan led the way back toward town, and Robin was thankful for the walk. He needed to move after that heavy but amazing lunch.

The street was lined with trees, and as they approached the center of town, Johan led them through the beer garden in the park, where they found a number of their group. Robin got them moving, and they continued on to their meeting spot right in front of the McDonald's, probably one of the only ones in the world with a facade done in Siena marble. The group lined up to use the bathroom while Johan got the bus, and Robin then got everyone loaded and ready to go. He only hoped they didn't have a stop half a dozen times to use the restroom.

"We're heading to Freiburg in the Black Forest region. This is one of my favorite stops. The center of town is somewhat unique, and there is plenty to explore both in town and in the forested hills above." Robin checked that everyone was present while he spoke and signaled to Johan that it was time to go, receiving a saucy grin and maybe even a leer in return. Robin felt himself flush as he sat down, and then they were on their way.

ROBIN WAS exhausted by the time they reached Freiburg, had dinner, and then got everyone into their rooms. Albert had booked a single room for him and Johan to share, which seemed to be the new norm for the trip.

"What do you expect?" Albert said when Robin called him. "I run on tight margins, and you can save me the room expense." He sounded snippy.

"What's gotten into you?" Robin asked. Albert usually wasn't so short and pissy.

"Nothing." He sighed softly. "I have another tour that I might have to cancel because there isn't enough interest. I have a few people who want to join and I'm working on it, but things are tight right now. No one wants to go on a gay tour any longer. Everything is getting so… normal now. They don't think there's a need, and maybe they're right." Albert sounding down was a completely new experience.

"It's going to be fine." Unfortunately there was little that could be done at this late juncture. It was already summer, and most people had already made their bookings. "You always figure something out." He'd intended to give Albert grief because he'd always had his own hotel room before, but there was no purpose now. Robin liked his job and wanted to keep it. "I'll call if I need anything, but otherwise, the tour is going fine." He ended the call to let Albert figure things out before lying back on the surprisingly comfortable bed in the spartan hotel room. Johan had gone out with Oliver, Javier, and Grant, but Robin didn't have the energy. He groaned as he got off the bed and cleaned up, then climbed beneath the sheets and closed his eyes.

He must have fallen right to sleep, because when he woke, he was warm and an arm rested over his side, a hand on his belly. Robin turned to find Johan asleep next to him, or mostly asleep. Part of him was most definitely awake, pressing to Robin's butt. He smiled and yawned, too tired to do anything about it, and what the hell? It was the most intimacy he'd experienced in months, and he liked that Johan held him, even if it was in his sleep.

Robin had requested a room with two beds for them, but this had been the only one available. He hadn't made a big deal out of it, not after the night before. But what surprised him was how easily Johan seemed to want to be next to him and how much better Robin slept being held by him. Sleeping with Mason had always been a huge ordeal. He snored loudly enough to reanimate a cemetery, and he tossed and turned all the damned time. Robin had hardly ever gotten a good night's rest when they'd slept together, but with Johan, things were very different.

"Go to sleep," Johan rumbled in German. Robin wasn't even sure if he was awake at all.

"I can't." Robin rolled over to face Johan, whose eyes cracked open. "Tomorrow is market day, and that means standing in the center of town for hours and making sure everyone finds what they want. Then to-morrow evening I'm supposed to lead a hike up into the forest above the town. I've done it before, and it always knocks me out."

"Then go to sleep and rest. They deserve the best of what you have to give." Johan stroked his arm gen-tly, and Robin closed his eyes.

"What if I'm getting too weak to do this anymore?" Robin asked, giving voice to the ever-present fear. The heart they'd given him was the best match they could have hoped for… or so the doctor had told him. But lately fatigue had set in, and he was worried that this was the start of the end for him.

"You aren't. I think this whole thing with Mason is getting to you." His tone made it clear that Johan didn't care for Mason at all. Somehow, that made Robin feel better. He'd have hated it if the two of them had hit it off and become friends or something. Just the thought sent the weirdness scale through the roof, and Robin shuddered. Johan must have thought he was chilled, because he settled even closer.

"Do you think it strange that we're sleeping like this?" Robin asked. "We aren't lovers, but…." Some-times he wondered why he had to question everything. There were people he knew—his brother Erik, for one—who never questioned anything. He took things as they came, and Erik was happy because of it. Robin wished sometimes he could be more like that and not worry or question everything.

"I don't know. Maybe it is." Johan shrugged and pulled him closer. "Stop asking so many questions. It's the middle of the night and you need to sleep. I need to sleep." Johan yawned, and Robin closed his eyes, resting his head on the pillow and trying to figure out what he was going to do. "Maybe we take the bus and park it at the base of the mountain. Let them walk up and back, but not quite so far."

"Good idea." Robin finally relaxed and let his worries go. He had a tour to lead, so instead of concentrating on what was in his head, he listened to the soft sounds of the night on the cobbled street from outside the open hotel room window. "Thanks, Johan."

CHAPTER 3

"Robin."

The word tickled the outside of his consciousness.

"Yeah," he muttered, cracking his eyes open. "It's still dark."

Johan gently shook his shoulder. "We have a problem."

A thump awakened Robin the rest of the way, and he jumped out of bed, tugged on his pants, and raced out into the hallway. Half the group was standing there, glaring at Billy and Kyle's door. "Go back to bed," Robin told them, and the others filed into their rooms. Robin knocked quietly on the door, and Kyle opened it, a tissue held to his nose.

Kyle stepped back so Robin could enter the room. Clothes lay over everything, hanging on the lamp and scattered on the floor. Billy sulked on the edge of his bed, looking down at the floor, hands cradling his head.

"Does either of you want to explain? It's supposed to be quiet at this hour. So, what's going on?" Robin needed to try to diffuse this situation so the hotel didn't complain. Albert wouldn't be happy if he had to find another Freiburg hotel.

"It was nothing," Kyle said, pulling the tissues away from his nose.

"You do realize that I have the authority to eject you from the group for bad behavior. That means that when we leave, I have every right to keep you from boarding the bus, and you'll have to get yourselves back to Frankfurt for your flight. Everything you've paid will be forfeited and you'll be on your own until then." Robin didn't want to do any of that, but if they didn't behave, he wasn't going to let them ruin everyone else's trip. "I need some answers."

"Billy has been drinking way too much, and…." Kyle glared at his friend. "And it needs to stop. He's drunk most of the time, and he can't act like anything other than an ass." Kyle put his hands on his hips, staring as Billy drew into himself.

"Whose clothes are these?" Robin asked.

"They're mine. Billy was angry when he came back from his latest round of drinking and I wasn't waiting up for him." Kyle seethed under his relatively calm words.

"Get them picked up and put away," Robin said to Billy. "I must say, this is terribly childish behavior on your part and doesn't reflect well on your best friend either. Both of you need to get to bed and sleep it off." Robin went to the door. "Billy, I want to talk to you in the morning before any of us goes anywhere. And you damn well better be sober." Robin left the room, noting a gallery of eyes peeking out of doors. He went right back to his room, closed the door, and sat on the edge of the bed.

Johan came out of the bathroom, then turned out the light and got into bed before soothing Robin in next to him.

"What are you going to do?" Johan asked once they were settled, his arm sliding around Robin. Robin's skin heated, but he didn't move and continued to face away from him. This was nice and all, but he was scared. How would Johan react when he found out Robin had such a short life ahead of him? Mason had run… so why should Robin expect anyone else to stick around? He shifted farther away, and Johan rolled over as well, the warmth fading.

"I never realized that part of this job would turn out to be counselor and even arbitrator. I had a couple who decided they were going to divorce once. They ended up completing the tour without speaking a word to each other for the rest of the trip. It was abysmal and affected everyone in the group." That had been the second tour of the season, and he'd never been so happy to say goodbye to people in his life. "I'll talk to them both in the morning." He closed his eyes and tried to go back to sleep, but found himself listening for any noise from the next room, though he finally drifted off.

Robin woke feeling stiff and nearly as tired as he'd been when he went to bed.

Johan was already up. He came out of the bathroom dressed and ready for the day. "I was quiet and hoped you could sleep a little longer. I'm heading down to breakfast." He left the room, and Robin pushed the covers down, checking the time and getting himself moving.

Everyone was at breakfast, including Kyle and Billy, sitting at separate tables and taking turns glaring at each other. Robin rolled his eyes and sat down with Johan, hating what was sure to come next. Of course, the incident the night before was the source of conversation and gossip, with plenty of supposition and no facts.

"Did you sleep at all?"

"Some," Robin admitted.

"The market is just a few blocks away. Take them all down, and they can go through the cathedral and peruse the stalls and town on their own if they'd like. Then you can rest for a little while if you want."

Robin nodded and got a roll and some juice. There was also a meat and cheese board, and he got a small assortment, then ate while pondering. What was he going to say to Billy? How should he handle that situation? And what should he say to Johan? Things were a little weird. Johan had held him for much of the night for the last two nights, but was that some pity thing or did he really like him? Maybe it was the way Johan slept when he shared a bed. He needed to talk to him as well but was kind of scared in case Johan was just being nice. Robin bit some of his hard roll and chewed slowly, not even realizing that he was holding the rest of the roll in midair.

"You must be really deep in thought," Mason commented as he passed, then leaned close. "You only do the ignore-the-entire-world thing when you're really trying to figure something out." He moved on before Robin could retort.

"Sometimes I want to smack that guy," Johan whispered.

Robin dropped his roll on his plate, giggling to himself and then laughing out loud. He had no reason to other than the release of tension and confusion. He probably looked demented, but it felt good to laugh. He didn't care that the others saw him. The stress relief felt too danged good.

Robin figured he'd talk to Billy now, and maybe he could speak with Johan tonight.

"I have a few announcements," Robin said, standing once he finished eating. "You have most of the day free to look around the town. There is some interesting shopping, and the market will take place around the cathedral, which will be open, so be sure to go inside. Also walk around it and look at the water spouts. The medieval carvers certainly had good imaginations. Lunch is on your own, and there are wonderful cafés and pastry and sandwich shops. Food is also available at the market. We'll meet here at five, when Johan will drive us out of town, and we'll hike up into the forest. It's beautifully stunning how quickly the area goes from city to nature. The name of the game is to enjoy yourselves." Robin caught Billy's gaze, and he colored and nodded.

Slowly the others got up and left the breakfast room. Robin stayed behind and motioned Billy over, waiting for him to sit down.

"Do you want to tell me what's going on?"

Billy shrugged, and Robin crossed his arms over his chest. "Kyle is…."

Robin shifted his weight, but otherwise stood still and quiet.

"Sometimes he makes me so angry."

"Why? He's your best friend. At least that's what you guys said when you got on the bus."

Billy sat back like he was going to clam up, and Robin waited him out. He knew this game well and was a master at waiting others out. "Sometimes he's so damn blind." Billy clenched his fists.

"What is he blind to?"

"Come on. I know you can figure things out even if he can't. What do I have to do to get Kyle to see me?" He crossed his arms over his chest. "I thought coming on this trip and sharing a room with him for over a week would… spark something. Instead, he acts like he always did, and…."

Robin leaned closer. "You're telling me you have feelings for him?"

"God." Billy shook his head, burying his face in his hands. "I have for a long time, and I hoped he liked me too, but…."

"Have you told him or done anything to make him see how you feel? Or are you drinking like a fish to bury your feelings, and all that did was make things worse?" Robin had a pretty good picture now of what he thought was going on. He sighed softly and nodded as he came to a decision. "Okay. As far as the tour goes, I suggest that you stop drinking. Switch to something else, because there will not be a repeat of last night."

"That's it?" Billy asked.

"Yes. You're an adult, so act like it. As for Kyle, you have to work things out with him. You two still need to room together. There aren't extra rooms in any of the hotels," Robin said, figuring he was done.

"You won't say anything about…?" Billy whispered.

"About what?" Robin asked. "As long as there is no repeat, I don't remember anything."

They joined the rest of the group, and Robin led them out of the hotel and along the cobbled streets to the old town center. He got everyone oriented and explained a little about the area where they were. They seemed excited to explore, and he didn't keep them too long. Once he made sure there were no questions, Robin went back up to his room, took off his shoes, and lay down on the bed. He'd taken his medication and just needed to try to make up for some of the lack of sleep from the night before.

He woke a couple hours later feeling somewhat better and more clearheaded. Johan hadn't come back upstairs, so Robin washed his face and brushed his teeth to freshen up before leaving the room. He headed down the cobbled streets of the old city center toward the cathedral and the market, smiling in the warm sunshine as the children played in the Bächle, little channels of fresh water running through the old city center streets.

Freiburg was unique in that it still had the remains of the medieval water supply. At that time, they channeled water from the river and ran it through a system of canals about a foot wide alongside the streets. Now, the water gurgled and shimmered in the sunshine as it flowed on its merry way. Robin loved how something so ingenious as a way to preserve some of the town's history made it so unbelievably quaint. And all he had to do was follow the water. It led him to the center of town and to the cathedral, where the town market was in full swing.

"Are you feeling better?" Johan asked as he strolled up to him. "I stayed away so you could rest." His expression was earnest and kind, filled with concern.

"I'm fine. A few hours of rest helped a lot." Robin looked around, unsure what to do now.

"Come on. There's some amazing fruit over here, and they have fresh wurst and *frites*. All kinds of things."

Robin bought some fruit and a little cheese, along with a loaf of bread, while Johan went off in search of something interesting to drink. They found a bench in the shade of the cathedral and set out their bounty in a makeshift picnic of amazing proportions.

"Break off some bread," Johan instructed, and cut some cheese into slices for him before pulling out the fruit. "I noticed that you don't eat a lot of fried food."

Robin shook his head. "It's… I need to watch what I eat so I don't put extra strain on my heart. So I try to eat lean foods and plenty of fruit and vegetables. It's harder over here because German food is heavier, but I love it. And pommes are the food of the gods." He took a bite of the cheese and bread, then sipped the Schorle Johan had found for him. "So much of my life revolves around that." There were some things he couldn't get away from no matter how much he wished they were different. The fact that he lived his life on borrowed time with a heart donated by someone else was something he could never get away from.

"What's it like to have gone through all that?" Johan asked.

Robin shrugged, shifting his gaze toward the top of the cathedral and its towers. "The surgery I don't really remember, other than the waiting and my parents hoping and praying. I was out of it a lot, and I had pretty much accepted that it seemed likely that I was going to die. Then they found a heart… an accident victim, or so I'm told. I don't know anything more about him other than he was about my age. When I woke up, I was in pain and had to take it easy for a long time." He swept his gaze over to the roofline and down the gothic-windowed wall toward the spire, rising toward heaven. "The doctors were afraid my body would reject it, so they watched me really closely, and I was on machines for a long time. But then I started getting better and stronger. My new heart beat on its own, and gradually they weaned me off a ton of stuff until I take just the medication I do today. It was a long road, and I know my mom and dad prayed a lot." Robin finished his bread and cheese, and nibbled on some amazing blackberries.

Johan broke off another piece of bread and handed it to him, along with more cheese. "What does your family think of you being over here? They have to be worried."

"My mom wants me to come home. She worries all the time. But I don't want to spend my life working in the family business, never seeing anything and being sheltered and coddled. What good is being given a life and not having the chance to live it? So I took this job, and I love it. I get to spend my summer in Europe and be on my own. My mom is German and my dad is American, so through a twist of fate and timing, I have dual citizenship. I can work here during the summer. After the tour season, I need to decide what I want to do. I can stay here because of my citizenship, or I can go back to America." Robin shrugged. "I don't know what I'm going to do."

"What about Mason?" Johan asked.

"He and I dated through college and afterward. He's part of the reason I looked for this job and came over here. My mom said I was running away, but it felt more like needing a change of scenery at the time." Robin finished his bread and cheese, declining with a gesture when Johan offered him more. "I wanted to see some of the world, and I had no idea that Mason was going to follow me over here. Though I should have suspected something." Robin smiled as he shook his head. "I've wondered in one of my wilder, more ridiculous moments if my mom had something to do with it. It would be like her to send someone over to keep an eye on me." He looked around, finishing up some of the fruit and drinking the last from his paper cup. He began packing up the trash for something to do.

"Do you really think she would do that?" Johan asked with a gasp.

Robin shook his head. "No. She'd never send him over here, but she probably knows he's here and she might have asked him to check on me."

"What's your mom like? You met mine." Johan grinned.

Robin thought a minute. "My mom shows love with food. That's the best way to describe her. She's short, under five feet, and a bit curvy, I guess. She has a quick smile and a wicked sense of humor, but only about some things." He tried to think. "She can be fierce. I swear the doctors found me a heart because they didn't want to face the unending wrath of my mother. When it comes to us, she's a lioness, without a doubt." He smiled slightly. "I bet my mom would love you." He reached out to gently stroke Johan's dark, soft hair without really thinking about it. Robin realized what he was doing and pulled away.

"But she doesn't let go well?" Johan asked.

Robin shook his head. "That's just about me. She's protective, and that means she wants to keep me close and keep me from hurt and stuff, I guess. She worries, but I have to make my own decisions. She's a mother. I bet she's a lot like yours in some ways."

"Yes." Johan smiled and gathered the rest of the trash. "This was a nice… bench picnic." He stuffed the paper in the bag and found a trash can to drop it all inside. Then he waited for Robin to join him. "What do you want to do? It's a beautiful day, and the group is out and about."

"Maybe a little shopping?" Robin offered. "There are some wonderful antique shops here, and I usually don't take the time to look around." He never had anyone to really go with before, and Johan seemed to like the idea. Robin checked his watch. "I have about an hour and then I should go back so I can confirm arrangements for our next stops."

They wandered for a little while, looking in some shops and enjoying the sunshine and warmth, until Johan tensed, his gaze following a group of large men in leather and dark clothes.

"What is it?"

"Did you hear them?" Johan asked. "They're talking about looking for some fags to bash. They apparently heard that there was a group in town and are spoiling for a fight." Johan pointed toward the hotel. "You get back and tell the hotel what's going on. I'm going to round up our people and get them out of here." Johan swore under his breath, a steady stream of German that turned the air eight shades of blue.

"Let's go."

"Robin," Johan growled.

"This is my group and I'm responsible." Robin headed for the square, and Johan passed him, leading him away from the main route and through smaller streets.

The market was still going on, and he found the four ladies at a sausage booth. "I'll tell them." Robin peeled away and hurried over as Johan continued through the market. "Get your food and go back to the hotel. There's a group of men that Johan thinks is going to cause trouble. I have to find the rest of the guys." He took a deep breath to calm his pounding heart.

"The three of you go back. I'll help Robin," Margaret said, and took off with Robin, holding his arm. "Now we'll look like a regular couple, if you know what I mean." She turned to walk to the right. "Billy and Grant are over there, and so are Oliver and Javier. I'll send them back. You see if you can find the others. Oh, there are Gerald and Harold. I'll send them back too."

"I'll find Mason and Kyle." God, Robin hoped they were together.

He didn't find them in the market and went to check the cathedral, quietly stepping inside to see if they were looking around. He didn't spot them and went back out to circle the market. The men were muscling their way through the crowd of people. Robin heard their threats and bravado and did his best to stay away from them, heading around and back to the edge of the market where he'd left Johan.

Margaret was there waiting for him. "Any luck?" she asked.

Robin shook his head. "I didn't see Johan either."

"We should go to the hotel. They could be there waiting for us."

Robin agreed, and they walked back that direction, down a side street. Everyone was gathered in the lobby, talking over one another.

"We called the police per Mr. Krause. I explained what was happening, and they said they could add a patrol to the market," the clerk said, seeming quite nervous and upset, and hung up the phone with a shaking hand. "We don't get this sort of thing in our town."

"It's not your fault." Robin turned to the group. "Please settle down. Has anyone seen Johan, Mason, or Kyle?"

"Mason and Kyle were together the last time I saw them," Javier said. "That was probably an hour ago. I'm not sure where they went."

"You can use the breakfast room if you'd like," the clerk offered, weaving through the group and opening the door.

Everyone filed in and sat down. They didn't really have a restaurant, but the clerk passed out glasses of water, which Robin was grateful for, taking one and wandering back into the lobby, pulling out his phone to call Johan.

"Where are you?" Robin asked as soon as Johan answered. "Did you find Mason and Kyle? They were seen at the market an hour ago."

"The market is breaking up, and the men are gone now. I'm on my way back. I haven't seen either of them. Do you have mobile phone numbers in your papers? Have you tried calling?"

"I'll see if I can raise Mason." Robin disconnected. He didn't remember if he still had Mason's number in his phone, but he checked and found it. He dialed and didn't get an answer, wondering if Mason's phone had been switched so it could receive calls in Europe. He tried multiple times, as Johan hurried up to the hotel. "I should have thought of this sooner, but I didn't."

"Anything?" Johan asked, but Robin shook his head.

"I tried calling Kyle, and he didn't answer either," Billy explained as he hurried in from the other room, pacing back and forth. "I'm going to try to find them." He muscled past them and out onto the street.

"Billy, please stay here." Even as Robin said it, he wondered how he could keep anyone from his group inside for the rest of the day. "The market will be torn down soon, and then the square will clear out. Saturday night is for cafés, restaurants, and that sort of thing. Nothing else is going to be open."

"It doesn't matter. I have to find him." Billy started off, and Johan followed after him.

"He can't go alone," Johan said as he disappeared from view.

Robin groaned, returning to the rest of the group.

"What do we do now?" Lily asked. "I don't want to sit in here for the rest of the day."

"Once we get everyone back, we'll get in the bus and go up into the forest. We'll move up our itinerary a little and get out into nature for a while. You can go on up to your rooms, or you can stay here. Either way is fine."

Robin went to the front door to look out. Of course, no one was coming back yet, and it was all he could do to stop pacing and sit down. He decided to confirm the arrangements for the rest of the trip. It needed to be done and would give him something to do. Robin went up to the room, got his folder, and returned to the lobby to make his calls where he could watch the front door.

No one came or went. The conversation in the other room was subdued to the point where Robin could barely hear it.

He had confirmed all his reservations and hung up the phone when Kyle stumbled into the room.

"Oh God." He dropped his phone on the seat and hurried over to him. "Kyle." Robin escorted him into the other room and sat him down. The buzz of conversation turned to chaos in seconds. "Get me some napkins." He motioned to the table, and Grant rushed over, handing them to him. "What happened? Are you all right?"

Kyle nodded and dabbed his bleeding nose and cut lip. "Some guys found me. I was outside a small shop behind the cathedral, just looking at the buildings. They taunted me, and I tried to get away. One of them took a swing at me while another hit me hard. I kneed one in the nuts and knocked down the other. I was able to run away and found my way here."

"We should call the police," Grant said.

"No." Kyle pulled the napkin away from his face. "It's just a bloody nose, and they got worse than they gave."

Billy pushed through the crush of people and engulfed Kyle in a hug, holding him tightly. "You scared me." Billy shook more than Kyle, and Robin backed away, motioning for the others to do the same. "I was looking for you and tried to catch up when I saw you." He continued hugging Kyle. "Let's go up to the room so we can get you cleaned up. Mason is still out there, and Johan was looking for him."

Billy got Kyle to his feet and led him to the stairs. Robin figured it was best to let them be alone. He'd talk to them both later.

Mason wandered into the hotel once they'd left, whistling happily to himself.

"Where have you been?" Oliver asked as soon as he spotted him.

"I was in town, taking care of some business," Mason explained with an unusually happy expression.

Robin narrowed his gaze. That particular smile usually meant Mason had been up to no good. It was the same one Mason had a few times when they were together.

"Some men were in the market looking for trouble. Kyle was accosted, but he's okay. We got everyone else back here but couldn't find you. I tried calling."

"You were worried about me. That's so sweet," he whispered.

Damn that smile. Robin wanted to punch it off Mason's lips.

"Don't be a smartass," Robin snapped. "As soon as Johan returns, anyone who wants to is going for a hike in the Black Forest. We thought a little time in nature would be good." Robin turned toward the door, hoping Johan would appear, but he didn't, which only added to Robin's tension. He hoped Mason would decide he wanted to stay in town to conduct more "business," whatever that was.

Johan finally returned, and Robin snapped, hugging him hard as he sniped at him for taking so long and not returning his messages.

"I am sorry. I was with the police. They have arrested the men for being disorderly and making threats. It is safe now." He patted Robin on the back.

"They got Kyle. He wasn't hurt badly and got back here a little while ago. He and Billy are up in their room." Robin smacked Johan's shoulder. "You should have stayed here."

"Mason?"

"Came back on his own. Didn't know anything was wrong." Robin backed away. "Let's get going. I think we need some fun and a touch of nature and fresh air after all this."

Johan agreed, and Robin got the message around that the bus would be leaving in fifteen minutes for whoever wanted go. Thankfully, Mason didn't come. To Robin's surprise, Billy and Kyle got on the bus. They sat together and didn't say anything, but they were there. Everyone else came, and they got on their way.

THERE WAS nothing like a few hours of quiet in the forest. The path was paved, but they'd been surrounded by dense forest, the ground covered with leaves, the air heavy and still, scented with leaves, earth, and even a few late-flowering shrubs near the breaks in the canopy.

"I love how the light dances when the leaves move," Robin told Johan as they headed back to the bus. He'd given the others some time on their own, though Billy and Kyle stayed close and came back with them. They got on the bus and sat in the back, talking quietly to each other.

"Do you think he's going to be okay?" Robin asked.

Johan shrugged. "I don't know. But I will talk with him." The haunted darkness in Johan's eyes sent a chill through Robin. He turned away to give him the privacy of his own thoughts.

"I love coming up here," Robin said, looking out over the valley to the city laid out below, with the cathedral dominating the skyline. "Can you picture it? The cathedral was built eight hundred years ago, and it's still awe-inspiring." He tried to imagine how someone who had only seen single- or two-story buildings at most would feel about something so large and grand. It took his breath away.

Johan got up from his driver's seat and walked toward the back of the bus. Robin followed him with his gaze as Johan checked one of the windows. After a few seconds, Billy came up and sat next to Robin.

"He's going to be okay," Robin said to try to reassure Billy.

"Yes, he is. I think things are going to be fine." Billy turned to watch them, and Robin continued looking outside at the view until Johan returned to his seat. Billy hurried back to Kyle as the others returned, climbing onto the bus to head back to town.

DINNER WAS subdued to say the least. Robin had called Albert to let him know what had happened before he went down to dinner. Albert had been furious and said he'd reconsider Freiburg as a stop on any tours for next season.

"If it's getting dangerous, I don't want to bring anyone else there." He was angry, though Robin ended up calming him down.

"Everyone is okay. Kyle wasn't hurt badly, and the police have the men in custody. We took the tour to the Black Forest, and tomorrow we're leaving." There was little else they could do at this point, and Robin was just happy to be putting this stop behind them.

No one went out after dinner. Instead, they lingered in the restaurant, talking and drinking before making their way back for the night. Robin had a drink himself, which was unusual, but he had to have a talk with Johan that he wasn't looking forward to.

"It's a nice evening," Johan said as they walked back to the hotel, and Robin nodded, shoving his hands in his pockets. "What's going on?"

"We need to talk, and I…." Robin paused on the corner, the street empty and quiet. "The last few nights have been nice…." He wiped his head. "I don't know

what's going on or what you think is happening, but…."
He stepped back when Johan reached for his hand.

"Did I do something wrong?" Johan asked.

Robin shook his head. "It's…." He started walking toward the hotel again, each footstep seeming heavier than the last. "There are things you don't know."

"So tell me." Johan caught up to him in a few strides, walking next to him on the cobbles. They moved to the side as a car rumbled down the narrow street, the tires *thunk*ing repeatedly on the stones.

Robin shook his head again, not wanting to have this conversation on the street.

They arrived at the hotel and went up to the room. Robin closed the door and sat on the edge of the bed. "Look. I need to explain something. I told you I got a new heart…. Well, most people are lucky if they make it through the first year, and my transplant was six years ago. I have six or maybe eight years left." He swallowed. "Mason told me that was part of why he broke things off."

"And you think I'll do that same thing?" Johan asked, aghast.

"No. That's just it. You're a better person than he is. You'd stay with me because that's the kind of guy you are. You'd look after me and put your life on hold for me." Robin needed to keep this short and sweet. Dragging it out wasn't going to help. "After the stuff with Mason, I knew I had to make the most of the time I had left, but I can't hurt someone else, not that way Mason hurt me." He lifted his gaze from his shoes. "You need to find someone who will be with you, someone you can grow old with. Because that isn't going to be me. I'm not going to grow old." His leg shook, but he knew what he was saying was right.

"Did Mason feed you that line of *Scheiße*?" Johan asked. "That man is a *Schweinehund*."

Under normal circumstances, Robin would have smiled at the German curses. Calling someone a pig-dog in English didn't carry the same impact. "But what if he's right? How are you going to feel if in a few years, the person you love is gone?" He didn't even want to insinuate himself in his own thoughts. A little distance was the only way he could get the words out. "I know we haven't started anything, not really. You're a nice man, and you deserve something more than what I can give you." He took a deep breath. "Maybe it's best if we become friends and nothing else." Just saying the words hurt.

Johan was stunned, staring at him with his mouth open slightly. He took a step back toward the door. "Is that what you really want?"

Robin groaned. "Why does what I want matter? I probably should go back to Milwaukee and work in my parents' bar. It would make them happy." He leaned forward, his head in his hands.

"Is that what you want? Not what you think you should do, but what you really want?" Johan knelt in front of him, and when Robin uncurled slightly, Johan placed his hand on his chest. "Here. Right here?"

"That's just it. What I want or what my heart wants doesn't matter. It's borrowed anyway. I got a new one from someone else, and it will only last so long. The odds of another are astronomical, and when my time is up… that's it." Robin placed his hand on top of Johan's. "I don't want to hurt you or anyone else."

Johan's hand stayed where it was. "You're the one who was hurt. Remember? Mason is the reason for all of this… foolishness." Johan's hand slipped away, the heat that built under it fading to nothing. "You have not answered my question. Is this what you want?" Johan stood, stepped toward the door, and placed his hand on the knob.

Robin opened his mouth to say that it wasn't, not really. He looked at Johan, trying to keep the hope out of his eyes. It truly was best if he didn't pursue this. "Johan, I…."

Johan opened the room door. "Does what I want matter in this?"

Robin blinked, hoping like hell to hold back the threatening tears. How could he already feel so empty about the loss of someone he'd never really paid attention to less than a week earlier?

Robin jumped when the door banged closed again. Johan covered the few feet between them in the blink of an eye and hauled Robin to his feet. Johan held him firmly, and Robin gasped when their gazes met. Before he could pull back, Johan kissed him, hard enough and with enough heat that he had to make sure his heart was still beating. Once the shock wore off, he let go and kissed Johan back, wrapping his arms around Johan's neck just to make sure this was real and to ensure he didn't end up in a heap on the floor.

Damn, Johan could kiss, and if this was the last one he got for the rest of his life, Robin knew he could now die a happy man.

When Johan pulled back, Robin gasped for breath for a second as Johan stared into his eyes. "Why don't you let me decide what I want to do. Okay? I can decide what I want just like you can, and there's no need to be noble on my account." He stroked Robin's cheek.

"But we've only known each other for… a couple of days, and we ended up in bed together." Robin snickered.

"We've known each other for longer than that." Johan bumped his hip. "Why do you think I asked for this tour and cut my hair and all? You said I looked like this Cousin Itt, whoever that is, and…."

Robin blushed. He hadn't thought he'd ever said that out loud. But then maybe he'd said it to Albert, who had a big mouth. Robin was a little embarrassed that it took Johan changing his looks for Robin to really notice him. He smoothed his hand over Johan's dark silken locks. "You're pretty sexy, and all the other guys think so too." Robin winked at him.

"I really don't care what the others think. There's only one person whose opinion I care about." He cupped Robin's cheeks.

"Yeah, but you could have anyone you wanted. Everyone—the guys, the ladies—they all think you're drop-dead gorgeous. Everywhere we go, you turn heads, and basically I try to disappear into the woodwork."

"Why do you think I noticed you?" Johan cocked his eyebrows. "You were always scurrying around in the background, taking care of everyone else and making sure they were having a good time. Then you sat outside on benches or in cafés, waiting while everyone else had fun. I thought maybe you should have some of your own once in a while." Johan closed the distance between them, pressing Robin back against the bed.

Robin tensed. "Are you sure about this?"

Johan slid his arms around Robin's waist. "How about you go ahead and take a turn in the bathroom? I'm going to get undressed out here, and I'll meet you in bed." Johan released him, and Robin stepped back.

"I know you've already seen me, but…."

"*Liebling*, we don't have to do anything you aren't ready for. There's no hurry for anything." Johan sat on the edge of the bed, and Robin slipped into the bathroom.

He stared at himself in the mirror over the sink. "Come on, heart, don't fail me now."

CHAPTER 4

ROBIN DIDN'T want to get out of bed. Everything was warm, comfortable, and perfect.

The alarm on his phone cut through Robin's contentment like a knife.

"We have to get up," Johan grumbled from behind him, still half asleep. As groggy as they both seemed, Robin would have thought they had been up half the night, but instead they'd stayed up talking until just after eleven.

"I know." Robin yawned and got out of bed. He hurried to the bathroom and closed the door behind him. It was strange after being naked under the covers all night. Still, he was self-conscious.

A knock sounded and then the door cracked open. "You all right?" Johan asked, stepping inside and winding his arms around Robin's waist. Johan was naked too, and there was no place for Robin to hide.

He closed his eyes. If he couldn't see himself, then maybe Johan wouldn't see him. Yeah, it was a little ostrichy, but it was what he needed to do to keep his anxiety from spiking.

"Liebling. Open your eyes. I don't know what you're so afraid of. I've seen you."

Robin felt Johan take a breath, waiting, and slid his eyes open.

"Maybe you need to look at yourself. So you have some scars. They aren't ugly. They're just there." He held him tighter.

"Mason never wanted to see me. I used to get undressed in the dark and got right into bed."

Johan sighed. "Was that for him or for you? Maybe he was just going along with what he thought you wanted." Johan met his gaze in the mirror.

Robin tensed, and it was on the edge of his tongue to deny it, but he couldn't. Robin wanted to think the worst of Mason, but maybe.... Blaming the failure of their relationship on Mason was easy, but they both had a hand in it. Well, Mason more than him, but he was partly to blame.

"Is this one from the heart transplant?" Johan asked, trailing a finger along the scar that ran down his chest.

"Yes. They had already opened my heart to try to repair it, and they had to go in again for the transplant. The scar used to be really angry, but over the years, it has pinked and faded somewhat. But it's all I see when I look at myself." Robin reached for his kit and pulled out a pill bottle. He took one out and popped it into his mouth. He downed it with water and leaned back against Johan. "I have to take those twice a day just to keep my heart working and my body from rejecting it.

I also take another one at night, and I have antibiotics that I can take if I get an infection and need a doctor to treat me. I don't take them without a doctor's authorization, but I have to have them on hand because other types could put me in danger."

"Then you know your body pretty well." Johan leaned closer to suck lightly at the base of his neck. "I'd like to get to know it too."

Robin shivered, then giggled, stifling it when he heard how stupid he sounded. "Yes, I do. I have to rest when I need to. Getting overtired puts a strain on me." Johan's warmth spread from where his front touched Robin's back to the rest of him.

"So is making love too much of a strain?" Johan asked.

Robin groaned as Johan's hard cock pressed against his butt. Jesus. He'd seen him at the spa, but not like this, and damn, the man was even more gorgeously proportioned than Robin had imagined.

"I can do most everything anyone else can do. Except I'm not going to be running marathons or going to the Olympics. I have to stay within my physical limits." He closed his eyes and let Johan play his body like a fine instrument. "I can't believe you like me… like this."

"Like what?" Johan whispered. "You need to let this 'I'm not good enough' thing go. It isn't helping you."

Robin turned around to face him, trying not to let his eyes slip southward. If he did, it was likely they were going back to bed, and then everyone on the tour would know what they were up to because they'd be waiting out front… for a while. "It's hard to let it go."

"You still hear Mason, don't you?" Johan asked, and Robin nodded. "Then tonight, after the night watchman tour, you and I will go to our room and I'll make you forget that ass ever existed." Johan pulled him closer, and Robin stilled, his expression hardening.

"How do you know we'll be sharing a room?"

Johan cleared his throat, and Robin knew he had him. He stepped away, crossing his arms across his chest. "When I asked Albert to make me your driver, I told him we could share rooms to save money." He had the decency to blush.

"I see." Robin wanted to be angry, but there was no way.

"I wanted to know you, and you seemed distant, so I pushed a little." Johan turned away and pulled open the door. "I will leave you to clean up." He patted Robin's ass gently, then left the bathroom, chuckling as he closed the door.

Robin was tempted to get Albert on the phone and read him the riot act. Not only had he gone along with this harebrained scheme, he'd been cheap enough to capitalize on it. The jerk. It seemed to have worked out, but Robin wasn't sure how he felt about being played. Then again, Johan had rescued him from a second night on that awful cot back in Freiburg....

He cracked the door open, peering out. "I don't know whether to thank you or smack you."

Johan smirked and turned his back, wagging his ass. "You could do both." He cocked his eyebrows, and Robin rolled his eyes, closing the bathroom door. There was no fucking way in hell he could be angry with him after that.

Robin shaved and brushed his teeth before washing up. After drying off, he wrapped the towel around his waist and left the bathroom for Johan. He passed him with a smirk, shutting off his hotness with the *snick* of the closing door. Robin dressed and packed his things. "I'll see you down in the lobby," he called through the door, and left the room.

Most of the group was in the breakfast room with their luggage already. Robin got something quick to eat and then collected keys, counting off each room to make sure he had them all. Mason and Grant weren't down yet. Billy and Kyle handed over their key, holding hands, and Robin hoped whatever had been between the two of them was worked out. Maybe Billy had mustered up the courage to tell Kyle how he felt.

"Johan will be down shortly to bring the bus around. We need to stay on schedule today. Rothenburg is always very busy, with a lot of people flooding the town during the day. My advice is to look around and do any shopping you want while the stores are open. Tonight we have the night watchman tour, and he'll take us all through the town. It's an amazing tour with a lot of explanation and history included." He pulled out his phone and called Mason. "Where are you?" Robin asked as soon as he answered.

"Out. I'll be back before nine," Mason said as though it was nothing.

"Then we'll be gone, and you can find your way on your own. The bus leaves at eight. That's printed in all the tour material." Fuck and blast. What the hell was Mason doing out already at this hour?

"Robin, come on." Mason used the tone that had always worked to get Robin to back down, and he actually found himself looking at his watch, figuring how he could make up the hour.

"Nope. Either get here in half an hour or be left behind." Robin ended the call and shoved his phone in his pocket, ignoring Mason's calls and messages.

Everyone else on the tour didn't need to be inconvenienced because of Mason's self-centeredness.

Grant came down the stairs looking like death warmed over. He slumped into a chair after getting two cups of coffee.

"What happened to you?" Billy asked.

"I went out with Mason, and…." Whatever else he was going to say ended up coming out as a groan.

"Did you bring your bags down?" Robin asked.

"I'll get them as soon as I'm alive again." Grant groaned again and drank some more coffee. Not that it would do him much good.

"Grant," Robin said, leaning a little closer so he could speak privately, wrinkling his nose. "You'd be better off taking a shower and getting your bags packed. The way you are now, no one is going to sit anywhere near you on the bus." He reeked of alcohol, stale cigarettes, and God knows what else.

Robin held his breath as he got Grant up and moving toward the stairs. Apparently their little know-it-all had let go of his inner geek and was making up for lost partying time. At the start of the tour, Robin would have guessed he'd be having hangover problems with Billy and Kyle, but they were now sober and bright-eyed.

"Finish eating and let's get the bus loaded."

Oliver stood, looking around. "Where's Mason? Everyone else is here. He had the room next to ours, and we heard him early this morning."

"Mason is out, apparently," Robin supplied, sitting back down.

Johan sat next to him with a cup of coffee and a light breakfast—well, a light one for him. Johan's plate was covered, and he ate with a hearty appetite. "I'm going to need my strength for tonight," Johan whispered just loud enough for Robin to hear.

He blushed and looked down at the tabletop, finishing his juice.

When he was done, Robin got his gear, and Johan went to bring the bus around. Robin met it and loaded his things while Johan got the bags. Robin checked off everyone as they climbed on board the bus. Grant still looked like hell, but he wasn't quite as disheveled, and the eau de gutter was thankfully absent.

Oliver and Javier approached, tension thick between them. "Come on," Javier said as he handed his bag to Johan, then tapped his foot as Oliver approached. He shook his head and got on the bus.

Robin pretended not to notice. "Morning, Oliver," he said in as normal a tone as he could muster.

Oliver patted him on the shoulder as if thanking him for his ignorance and climbed on the bus.

The others filed on, talking softly. As expected, Mason was the only one absent. Robin went to turn in all the keys and explained that Mason still had his and hadn't come back. He checked the time—already five after. He returned to the bus. "I'll give him five more minutes and then we go." They were blocking most of the relatively narrow street as it was and couldn't stay there for much longer.

"Will we really leave him behind?" Lily asked when Robin climbed on the bus as Johan closed the luggage hatches.

"Of course not. I never leave anyone behind." Robin turned to the group. "But sometimes people decide they don't want to catch the bus and want to make their own way to the next stop. There's nothing I can do about that."

Johan climbed on board, and the brakes released as Mason rounded the corner ahead, racing up the street, a pack bobbing on his back. Johan sighed and opened the door.

Robin stepped out. "Get your stuff."

Mason nodded as he passed the bus, explosive anger in his expression that Robin pretended not to see.

Robin waited a few minutes, then went up to Mason's room. "You have two minutes," he said from outside the door and turned to leave.

"You could have waited," Mason argued as he yanked open his door.

"Why should everyone have to wait because of you?" Robin got right in his face. "You're a selfish prick, you know that? And you need to learn that you will get nothing special from me. You were told the time, and it was in the itinerary that you were given. Now get moving." He held out his hand, and Mason stared at it. "Your key."

Mason handed it to him, and Robin went down the stairs and handed it to the man at the desk. "Thank you for everything."

Johan was waiting outside the bus for Mason to stow his bag. Robin got on and ignored Mason as he also climbed on. Johan closed everything up again, and they were finally off.

"THE FIRST time I made this drive," Robin said to the group as they rode, "I dreamed of what it would be like to live on one of these farms." He turned to look out the window. A steady landscape of tree-covered hills, valleys, and farmland had passed outside their window for the last hour. Some of the tourists napped, while others watched outside. "Then we passed into the valleys just like this one, and I wanted to live there, be part of a community that has been there for nearly a thousand years or more."

"You never could have," Mason sneered from his seat a few rows away.

Robin ignored him. *Let him sulk.* Besides, Robin didn't have to say anything. The dirty looks from Lily and Margaret assured him Mason wasn't going to get anywhere with the group.

"It was only a dream, of course, but it would be interesting." Robin sat back down and watched out the window himself, letting the bus grow quiet until they were ten minutes out of town. "Johan will be able to let us out near our hotel. Gather your bags quickly, and we'll take them right over. They will store them for us. Johan can only park there for ten minutes, so we need to be fast. Then he'll take the bus outside of town to the lot. Don't leave anything on the bus at all. Not this time." Robin waited for questions and then watched as they passed into Germany's best-preserved walled town. It was a tourist mecca because it was so amazing.

Most of the busloads of tourists hadn't arrived yet, which was why Robin had wanted to get moving as early as they had. Johan crept the bus through town, making careful turns, until they arrived at Hotel Maria Louise. It was in a beautiful medieval building with slightly crooked walls and a tile roof that looked original but probably wasn't, just made to look old. Painted green with red geranium flower boxes on all the windows, it was charming and quintessentially German.

Robin got off the bus and went inside. He checked in with the manager, who gave them a small room where they could put their luggage. Johan was nice enough to coordinate the unloading and placement of the luggage while Robin took care of the rest of the details. Then he returned to the group, which bristled with anticipation.

"I have maps for each of you." Robin handed them out. "Have fun. But I have a few things to say before I let you go. There are lots of things here designed to part you from your money. The medieval museums, and sometimes pickpockets. Just be careful. Lunch is on your own, and there are wonderful restaurants and great shops. Also, if I can give you a suggestion, there's a walkway in the wall and you can climb one of the towers. It's an amazing view."

"There's a Christmas store," Lily said with an excited grin.

"Yes. Käthe Wohlfahrt's is the original German Christmas store, and they started here. Enjoy yourselves and be back here by five o'clock at the latest. We can check in at three, and I'll be here with your room keys then. Enjoy yourselves, and have fun."

They hurried off to be part of the excitement, and Robin sighed, trying to decide what he was going to do with his day.

On his early tours, Robin had guided his groups through the town, pointing out the highlights—including the town hall, Glockenspiel, and what the various seals and crests meant on the buildings—but his groups had chomped at the bit to see the sights and shop on their own, so that was what he did now, and he left the tour to the night watchmen, who were more entertaining than he was.

Johan had already pulled the bus away, so Robin sighed again. It was too early to call his mom, and there was nothing he needed from Albert. Plus, Robin had already confirmed the rest of his tour stops. He loved Rothenburg and decided to wander around after resting for a while. He'd been more tired on this tour than he had on previous ones, so he figured a few minutes' break was in order.

"I was hoping you'd wait for me," Johan said as he strode inside and sat next to Robin about ten minutes later. "The bus is parked and locked in the lot. I tipped the attendant, and Karl will take good care of it. What do you have to do?"

"Nothing," Robin answered. "Call my mother later so she doesn't worry."

"Then come on." Johan took his hand and stood.

"Where are we going?"

"Käthe's. You can find something for your mother and have it shipped to her. She will think you are the best son ever." Johan smiled and led him down to the main road and into a Christmas wonderland. Ornaments, nutcrackers, smokers, and other decorations, flickering lights, and Christmas music—everything meant to transport you to another world. It even had the slight scent of baking cookies and cinnamon.

"I haven't been in here in a long time." Not since his first visit before the start of the season.

"They have some wonderful things." Johan walked with him through display after display, past wooden and crystal ornaments. "What sort of thing would your mother like?"

"Mom cooks, but her passion is baking." Robin stopped in front of a display of incense smokers, including a lady baker. Most of the designs were quite traditional, so seeing that particular design was unusual. Robin liked it, so he took the tag to the register. When they brought him the item, he paid for it and arranged to have it sent. That wasn't something he usually did, but Käthe's was reputable and would make sure it was shipped properly.

They left the store and wandered through the town. "Do you want to find lunch, get something to eat outdoors?" Johan offered.

"What I want is something fresh and light." Robin could go for a nice salad plate. "Please, nothing fried or heavy." He patted his belly as though to make it an excuse. "I need to try to keep my diet light. A lot of fat and cholesterol is bad for me. The healthier I eat, the better off I am." He hoped Johan would understand.

"It is no problem." Johan led the way to a hotel and spoke to the host on duty. They were taken to a table outdoors under an expansive tree. "I like it here. Tourists come here a lot, but the food is very good." Johan leaned forward. "Trust me?" he asked, and when the waiter approached, Johan ordered a large salad with their house dressing, some bread, cheese, and a meat plate, as well as an apple Schorle for Robin and a glass of white wine for himself.

"That's perfect, thank you," Robin said. He sipped from his glass when the server brought it for him.

Johan nodded and smiled. When Johan turned to watch people in the square, Robin took the chance to watch Johan. His scruff-covered jaw and cheek glistened in the sun, as did his jet-black hair. Robin thought he was the most perfectly stunning and handsome man he'd ever laid eyes on. Johan turned back to him, his eyes sparkling in the ray of sunshine that dappled through the trees.

"Robin," Billy said as he rushed up, weaving through the other tables until he reached them. Kyle approached more slowly. "My money is gone. I was in the Christmas store...." He pointed across the way.

"I was going to pay for something for my sister, and I didn't have it."

Robin slid over so he could pull up a chair. "Are you sure you had it with you when we left this morning?"

Billy nodded. "I need to get some more. I hid some in my luggage at the hotel."

"Okay." Robin stayed calm and hoped the feeling would help Billy. Kyle got a chair and sat next to Billy, holding his hand. "Is anything else missing? Credit cards, ID?" God, he hoped his passport hadn't come up missing. That would be a pain to replace.

"No." Billy pulled them out of his front pocket.

"All right. How much is missing?"

"A hundred euros." Billy sounded heartbroken, giving Robin the idea that he was budgeting pretty closely on this trip.

"You can go back to the hotel and ask the clerk to let you in the room to get to your luggage, or you can find an ATM machine. They will dispense euros, and your bank will do the currency conversion. It's up to you." Robin truly wished this sort of thing didn't happen. "I'm sorry about all this."

Billy nodded and stood. "Thanks, Robin." He and Kyle walked off together.

Robin shook his head. "Shit," he said softly under his breath as the server brought his lunch. "I hate when this happens." He suddenly wasn't very hungry and hoped there was something he could do to help.

"Eat. You cannot help anyone if you do not eat." Johan pushed the salad over, and Robin took a few bites. His hunger kicked in, and he ate more quickly. Johan passed him some bread, meat, and cheese, and Robin ate some of that as well.

"After we eat, I want to make sure he's gotten what he needs." Robin had made sure he had everyone's cell numbers in his phone so there was no repeat of what happened in Freiburg.

He sent a message, and Billy answered it right away. Kyle had apparently found an ATM and had helped him out. That warmed his heart a little. He liked that the two of them seemed to be getting closer.

A familiar voice drifted on the breeze, cutting through the myriad of others. "Get away!" Oliver and Javier stood apart, glaring at each other.

"That is a match made in *Hölle*," Johan commented. "They fight all the time."

Robin wished he could argue.

Javier stalked off down the sun-bleached cobbled street, and Oliver followed, his shoulders slumped. Robin wondered just how much longer they would be together at all.

"Do you think he's a rent boy?" Johan asked, following Javier with his gaze. "He sure acts like that." He turned his gaze back. "Maybe Oliver hired him to come on this trip with him because he didn't want to be alone."

Robin shrugged. "Oliver is attractive. Sure, he's a little older, but he has the gray-around-the-temples thing going on, and he's nice enough. If that's true, I'm sure he had a reason for it." Robin couldn't see why anyone would do something like that. But there was something about those two that he couldn't quite figure out. "Maybe it's a power thing. Oliver has it because he has the money, but Javier is too strong-willed to let anyone have power over him. So he gets impatient and rebellious. It sort of makes sense to me. What I don't understand is why they both allow it."

Johan sipped his wine. "That's because you are a nice guy who… well…." He set down his glass. "I think you have a different perspective on life than anyone else. You understand your own mortality and that we don't have forever." Johan looked around. "Everyone, all of them, go around as though they own everything and have all the time in the world. You know different. That's why you're here. At least that's what I heard you say." He reached across and took Robin's hand in his, sliding his thumb softly around the back in little circles. "Maybe you understand that too well."

Robin didn't know what to say. Maybe Johan was right and he'd let that get in the way. "Is that possible?"

Johan nodded. "If you let it get in the way of you being happy, I think it is." He continued holding his hand for a few seconds, and Robin closed his eyes, letting the connection flow between them. He hadn't felt this in tune, this close, to Mason until months into their relationship. And as he looked back on it, the spark had disappeared a long time before things ended.

A chair at their table moved, and Robin jumped. Mason had plopped himself down before Robin realized it.

"I see how things are," he sneered, and Robin tried to pull his hand back, but Johan held it.

"What you see is none of your business. You are Robin's ex, and from what I've seen, doing what you can to make him miserable. Knock it off." The growl from Johan was sexy as hell.

"What do you want?" Robin asked as Johan released his hand and Robin returned to his lunch.

"I saw you sitting here and thought, since you're our tour leader, that you might have some ideas on how to spend the day?" Mason cocked his eyebrows.

"You have the day on your own. Look around. Go walk the wall and climb the tower." Robin didn't look up from his food, hoping Mason would take the hint. He didn't. "There are museums and shops—just wander." It was becoming clear that Mason wanted someone to do things with, and Robin guessed the rest of the group had ditched him.

"You're the tour guide…." Mason tilted his head expectantly. "I thought you could show me around."

Robin glanced at Johan, who seemed resigned, and Robin stifled a groan. "Fine. Once we're done with lunch, I'll take you on a tour of the wall. We can walk it, and you can go to the top of the tower." Robin had no intention of climbing those steps. "How is that?" He was not going to be spending the rest of the day with his ex-boyfriend.

"Great," Mason said with a smile, then turned to Johan. "Don't you need to check on the bus or something?"

"Mason!" Robin snapped. "You will not be rude to anyone, and if you want me to show you the wall, then Johan is welcome to join us." He hoped Johan got the idea that he wasn't keen on being alone with him. Mason settled in his chair, and Robin sighed. "Let us finish our lunch and then we'll go." He glared, and Mason finally got the hint. He stood and dejectedly left. Robin looked at Johan. "I'm sorry. This is not how I wanted to spend the day."

"Mason is an ass, and you're way too nice." Johan smiled warmly. "But I won't fault you for that. I will be your watchdog, though, and I'm not going to let him wear you out." He tore a bite of his bread and tossed it into his mouth.

Robin finished his salad and had a little more bread and cheese. He drank his drink, and Johan paid the bill before Robin could stop him. Mason joined them as they left the restaurant, and Robin led the way to the wall.

"This is the medieval wall of the town. Parts of it were damaged in the war and repaired. You'll see commemorative stones for people and groups that helped sponsor the repairs. It has, of course, been renovated so tourists can walk it. It's definitely pretty impressive." Robin was careful where he stepped. The stone walkway could be a little uneven. "The towers and gates are original, though they've been repaired." He paused to look out the windows and noticed that Mason wasn't paying attention. "You wanted me to show you around."

Mason flashed him that pouty look he used when he wasn't getting his own way. "I wanted to be able to talk to you alone," Mason confessed.

Robin scowled. "Did it ever occur to you that I don't want to talk to you? I was the one to come home and find you in bed with someone else right before our trip to see my family. Then you had the gall to dump me." Robin clenched his fists. He had tried so hard to make it seem like things were normal that Christmas. "I thought I was going to crawl into a hole and die after that. But I dusted myself off and found this job over here while I nursed my broken heart, thinking I didn't deserve anyone else." He shrugged and held out his hand, which Johan took. "Now that I might have found someone else, you have decided that you're going to interfere."

"Why don't you go on your way and see to your own fun?" Johan suggested, motioning toward the nearest stairs.

Robin had already started walking in that direction when Mason called out.

"Do you really think I won't call your tour company and complain? I wonder what they'd say about the two of you going at it like rabbits."

Robin paused and turned around. "First thing, I have already informed the tour operator about you and your little stunt of booking my tour. They are none too happy with you at the moment. And as for the two of us being together… of the three other guides and drivers in the field right now, one pair is married. So I don't think the tour operator—or anyone else—is going to care who I sleep with." Robin chuckled. "Besides, I think he's been playing matchmaker all along." Robin rolled his eyes and took the first step down the stairs. "Have fun today, Mason. I'll see you back at the hotel." Robin descended the stairs and waited for Johan, who followed him down a few minutes later. "What did you say to Mason?" Robin asked as they headed back toward the center of town.

Johan shook his head. "Nothing too important. Just that he needed to mind his own business. I have lots of friends, and some of them know how to make things—and people—disappear." He grinned. "Now, let's go. We have some fun waiting for us while we can be alone. And I know a place with the best sweets. Think a cookie base, nougat, and hazelnuts, all covered in dark chocolate."

Robin's stomach rumbled from lunch, loudly enough for Johan to hear him. "Oops."

"I thought so. Come on. You are way too skinny." He led Robin slowly through the streets. The throngs of tourists fell away as they found themselves in a part of town few tourists saw. Medieval homes and businesses, narrow streets, and quiet greeted them as they strolled. "This is the way this town should be."

"They need money to survive."

"Yes. But could you imagine being one of the artists who discovered this place in the late nineteenth century? Walking through those gates into another world. It must have been breathtaking… and quiet, the town having slept, untouched, for over two hundred years."

Robin closed his eyes. It was easy enough to imagine, but he'd never thought of it. "I had no idea you had the soul of a poet… or maybe a philosopher." He leaned against Johan, letting the stillness wash through him.

They continued their walk until they found themselves on the square. Johan excused himself, then returned with a white bag and handed him a single chocolate confection in a ring shape. "Let's eat as we head to the hotel. It's about time to go back to work." Johan led the way while Robin took bite after bite of sheer chocolate-and-hazelnut heaven.

ROBIN SAT in the hotel lobby waiting for his group. He'd checked in for all the rooms and had worked up the assignments, so now he just had to sit and wait.

"I guess I'll go up to my room," Mason groused as he schlepped in.

Robin got his key and handed it to him after he got his luggage. Mason hauled it up the stairs. The bag looked exceedingly heavy, and Robin wondered for a second what kind of souvenirs he was collecting on his trip. If the bag weighed as much as it seemed, Mason wasn't going to get everything home.

"That was awesome," Billy said as he and Kyle came in arm and arm. Kyle got their bags, and Robin motioned to Billy.

"Did you tell him?"

Billy grinned and nodded. "All that stuff that happened gave me the guts, you know. I figured I could lose him if I didn't speak up. He and I are working stuff out." He blushed, and Robin got a pretty good idea of how they were going about that.

"That's good." Robin turned as Grant came in. He handed him his key, and Grant got his luggage and went on up. Kyle shuffled up the stairs after him.

"Poor Grant," Billy said, lightly clicking his tongue. "He had a thing for Mason, and that guy is a real jerk. They went out, Mason got Grant drunk, and then left him behind to meet with some guy in the club. Grant ended up finding his way back alone. He doesn't know where Mason got off to."

"So Mason didn't come back at all last night?" Robin asked, half wondering out loud. "Maybe he found some guy. He has a history of that."

"I figured you would know. Word has it that you guys dated for a while." Billy shook his head. "How could you stand it? He's a real slime." Billy turned to Kyle, who had come back down the stairs. "Are we all set?"

"Yes, hon," Kyle said gently and rejoined him. "Why don't we go get some coffee and a snack somewhere? We need to be back by five, but that's enough time. I don't want to waste a minute." He took Billy's hand and they took off, Billy waving goodbye as he hurried out the door.

Robin sat back down and called Albert. "What did you think you were doing?"

"Problem?" Albert asked.

"The guy you added, Mason, my ex-boyfriend, is causing a lot of trouble." Robin needed to have some backup from Albert. "He's a real jerk and thinks he can use the past we had to get what he wants. He was late getting to the bus so I almost left him this morning, and the others in the group don't like him either." There was some satisfaction in that.

Albert sighed. "He's paid for his tour, so unless he does something bad enough for you to kick him off…."

"Yeah, I know." Robin didn't want to do that unless he had to. "I wanted you to know. He threatened to report me because I didn't give him a personal tour. He actually threatened me because Johan and I are getting close." He rolled his eyes, and Albert squealed on the other end of the line.

"He told me he was interested," Albert said, his version of cagey.

"Yeah. Well, I'm not sure if I'm mad at you or not."

Albert snorted. "You saw him, and he was interested in you. I figured I was doing you a favor. So, enjoy and have fun. I've got another call coming in. Keep me informed about Mason. If he really causes trouble, I'll handle it."

"Thanks." All he really wanted was a little cover from Albert in case he felt he had to act.

Robin handed out the rest of the keys and got everyone settled. Johan went to check on the bus, and when he returned, he was nice enough to carry both their bags up.

By the time everyone had returned and had their keys, Robin was running late. "All right. We're going to head to dinner." He checked his watch and led the group down the street to a small restaurant where tables had been set up for them. Robin made sure everyone was seated and slumped in his own seat. God, he was so tired and winded. He'd hoped to be able to go on the tour that evening with the rest of them, but the day's activity was catching up with him. Maybe a nap for half an hour after dinner would help.

"We have to meet at eight for the tour, right?" Kyle asked from the next table.

"Yes." Robin handed out the tickets to each of them. "Meet in front of the town hall. The night watchman will take the tickets. This particular tour is in English. They have limited spots, and we managed to get most of them for tonight. So please be on time. If you're late, you're out of luck." Robin turned to Mason, who had the grace to appear sheepish.

"Are you coming with us?" Grant asked.

"Maybe." Robin turned to Johan. "Unless you'd like to go. There is only one extra ticket, and I've been on the tour." Robin wanted to give Johan the chance.

"It's something I've never done," Johan said.

Robin handed him the ticket. "Then have fun." A chance to catch his breath was probably a better use of his time. "You'll enjoy it." The thought of some rest was too good to pass up. He hoped he wasn't coming down with anything.

The servers brought salad plates, and the conversation in the room simmered around him as they all ate. Robin's hands began to ache a little when he was halfway through dinner, and he knew taking it easy after dinner was probably the wise decision. He ate lightly and made sure Johan would take care of anything the group needed before heading up to the room.

White curtains billowed from the open window, fluttering in the light breeze. The room was surprisingly cool, furnished with light wooden furniture, comfortable and nice. The bed called to him. Robin took off his shoes and lay down, closing his eyes. At first he didn't need any covers, but a chill set in and he climbed under the duvet, shivering. "Dammit." He most likely had a fever. Robin finally warmed up and slipped off to sleep.

The room was dim but not dark when he woke. Robin felt better, though his clothes were damp with sweat. He got up, opened his bag, and took a change of clothes to the small bathroom.

"Robin," he heard Johan say through the door.

"I'll be right out." Robin stripped off his damp things and hung them over the rod to dry before he put them into his dirty clothes bag. He dried off, put on fresh clothes, and stepped out. "Are you about to go?"

"Mason has decided he isn't going and gave me back his ticket. I thought I would see if you wanted to come, but you look very pale and your eyes…." Johan paused and sat down on the edge of the bed. "I'll make sure they get on their tour and then I'm coming back here. Do you have any medication you can take?"

Robin nodded, and Johan handed him his kit from his suitcase. "I'll take something for my headache and sit up awhile. You don't need to stay here with me." Robin found what he was looking for and took the pill. Then he sat back on the bed, his head and body propped up by the pillows, and turned on the television. "Please go have fun." He hated the thought that he was keeping Johan.

Johan leaned toward him to feel his forehead. "Is your stomach upset?"

"No. But my throat hurts a little." Robin cleared his throat, and Johan took his hand for a few minutes. "Go on. I'll be fine." He covered himself with the duvet and watched an action hero movie dubbed in German. Johan left the room as Robin settled in to rest for the evening.

What he didn't expect was for Johan to return less than an hour later with bottles of fruit juice and two covered foam cups.

"I brought you some ice to soothe your throat."

Robin sighed. He loved Germany and being here, but one of the hardest things to get used to was the lack of ice. Drinks were chilled but not cold, and while he'd gotten used to it, this was amazing.

After taking off the lid, Johan handed him the first cup and poured some apple juice for him.

Robin sipped, and the cold liquid soothed his parched throat. "You were supposed to go on the tour."

"I know. But I'd be worried about you the entire time." Johan took off his shoes and climbed onto the bed to sit next to him. Robin shifted closer, and Johan put an arm around him. Robin should probably be starting to work on his next tour, but damned if he felt like it. He reached for his phone and sent Albert a note that he wasn't feeling well and would let him know if he felt worse. Then he settled in, surrounded by Johan's warmth.

"I'm sorry," Robin said quietly, turning to Johan. "Tonight was supposed to be special, and I ruined it." He blinked and sighed. Damn it all. Part of him wished he'd mustered up the energy so he didn't disappoint Johan.

"It's all right." Johan held him tighter. "Sex is nice, but it isn't the end-all, be-all of life."

Robin leaned against him a little more, feeling his heart open to Johan a bit further each time he was with him.

"I don't want to disappoint you." He closed his eyes. Damn, this felt nice. He was safe and secure, or at least he felt that way. Robin drank a little more juice and relaxed while Johan watched the movie, which seemed to grow quieter as his eyelids slid closed.

"You haven't. I like being here with you."

Robin sniffed and tried to cover his emotions by clearing his throat. He wasn't sure if he was successful. "I don't see why. I'm not that interesting."

Johan scoffed. "You have experiences that no one else has. What you went through makes you totally unique, and you don't see it." He shifted slightly and turned off the television. "What were you like before you had the transplant?"

"Oh God." Robin thought back. "I remember that I was always tired, and my mom taught me at home for a number of years because she and my dad were scared that if I went to school with other kids, I'd bring home viruses and things that could make me sick. I couldn't run and play with the other kids, though I tried at each opportunity. I loved to be out and about, and it scared my mom and dad. I remember my grandma telling Mom that she and Dad couldn't shelter me and that I had to live whatever life I had to the most. Mom yelled at her, and they didn't realize I was listening." He lifted his gaze to catch Johan's eyes. "I used to spend so much time inside. I remember watching *The Cat in the Hat* cartoon and felt like those kids caught inside on a rainy day. Except every day seemed rainy for me."

"Wow. I don't think I can imagine not being able to go out and play with my friends. Mom and Dad had a large social circle because of the restaurant, and we used to have gatherings there all the time. We were closed one day a week, and we usually met friends that day."

Johan turned, and Robin knew he was going to kiss him. Robin backed away.

"Don't get what I have, okay? I don't want you to be sick too."

Robin wasn't expecting Johan to laugh.

"I've been sleeping next to you for days, and the last two nights you've burrowed next to me as though you were sucking up the warmth. I think if I'm going to catch something, I probably already have it." Johan kissed the top of his head. "Just relax and don't worry. You already look a little better and don't feel as warm as you did before. A good night's sleep will probably do wonders for you." Johan climbed off the bed and slipped on his shoes. "I'm going to go downstairs and make sure everyone makes it in all right. You just rest, and I'll be back."

Johan left him alone, and Robin took the opportunity to get ready for bed, then burrowed under the covers and turned out the lights. He fell right to sleep and barely stirred when Johan joined him.

At some point he woke to Johan's light snoring. His head was clear and his body aches were gone. Robin was grateful for that and stayed awake for a while, wondering how lucky he could get, meeting someone like Johan. He might be crazy to fall for him so quickly, and maybe sleeping next to Johan was a bad idea, but it felt right and… oh, to hell with it. How many chances would he get to be with someone as amazing as Johan? He wasn't going to let this opportunity slip through his fingers. Robin snuggled closer and closed his eyes, falling right back to sleep.

CHAPTER 5

JOHAN STOWED their bags as Robin followed Mason onto the bus. He wanted to check for the missing money, so Robin went down the aisle. He saw Mason lean into one of the seats and came up behind him.

"You found Billy's money," Robin said, and Mason stilled, then straightened up and handed Robin the cash. A hundred euros—exactly what Billy had lost. "Thank you. He's going to be so happy."

Robin left the bus and went back into the hotel. It wasn't until he reached the lobby that he wondered if Mason had been going to say anything or simply pocket the cash. Yeah, he wasn't too happy with his ex right now, but Robin liked to think Mason was a better person than that. But then again, he'd cheated on him, so why not steal as well?

"Billy," Robin said with a smile as he walked up to him. "Look what Mason found on the bus." He handed him the cash, and Billy broke into a grin. "It was on your seat. He was the first one on the bus, and he and I found it there."

"Awesome." Billy put his hand over his chest. "I—"

"It's okay. I know what it meant to you." Robin patted Billy on the shoulder, happy he could help him. "Go and get ready. We need to leave by eight for our trip to Munich. I have some amazing things planned for you there, including a day trip to Füssen to see the fairy-tale castle." He was excited and feeling much better.

"Are we going to Oktoberfest?" Kyle asked.

"That's in late September and into October. But if you want, you can walk over to the grounds. They should be setting up some of the beer halls already." Robin walked outside as the rest of the group lined up to get on the bus. "Did you all have a great time?"

"I loved how the town grew so quiet after dark. It was like a completely different place," Grant said as he boarded.

"That's why we stay overnight. It's the best time to get the real feel for the town, and seeing everything with the lights on is stunning." Robin counted everyone and climbed on the bus last, doing one final check before telling Johan they were ready to go.

"How long is the drive?" Lily asked.

"About four hours. Sit back and relax. There will be some beautiful scenery as we cross the countryside. We'll be crossing into Bavaria, and Munich is the capital. A lot of what we think of as German in the US comes from Bavaria—Oktoberfest and the maypoles, to name a few. The kingdom of Bavaria had its own royal line and government until German unification. After that, they still had a king, but he wielded no governmental power. The Wittelsbach family is still around. They are what is often referred to as unofficial royalty, and they maintain a number of royal residences, including one we will see when we go to Füssen. Hohenschwangau is owned and operated by the family. You'll see it up on the hill when we go tomorrow."

"Will they be there?" Billy asked. "I always wanted to meet royalty."

Kyle snickered. "Please, you're a big enough queen that royalty will pale in comparison."

Billy rolled his eyes and smiled.

Robin continued. "Much of Bavaria is Catholic. Unlike Rothenburg, which was largely Protestant. So the churches will be much more ornate on the inside. Protestants kept things simple, while the Catholics were more ostentatious."

"What about the war?" Grant asked.

Robin nodded. "Unfortunately, much of what you will see is a reconstruction. Much of the city was leveled during the war. You'll see before, after, and current photographs. They have done an amazing job of restoration, and you would be hard-pressed to even realize that everything isn't hundreds of years old. My advice is to concentrate on the great things you'll see and ignore how old or new it is." Robin thought for a second. "Munich has an amazing subway system, and you can easily get anywhere in the city. If you want to use the subway, let me know and I will be glad to explain how it works. It's a very German thing." He smiled and noticed that a number of people were starting to nod off, so he sat back down and let the bus go quiet.

The ride was pleasant. Billy and Kyle sat in the row behind him, and they asked a ton of questions about Munich and talked about the trip so far.

"Thanks again for finding my money." Billy turned to look at Mason without any mirth or pleasantry. "I don't think he would have been so keen to return it."

Robin scowled and flicked his gaze to Mason, who looked out the window, his jaw set and hard, and then back to Billy. "Why do you say that?"

Billy turned to Kyle, biting his lower lip.

Kyle nodded and nudged him slightly. "Go ahead. You need to tell him what you think you saw."

Billy swallowed. "We were in one of the shops that sold nicer things. They had some silver items in a case. They were very pretty and really expensive. I think they were antique. The case was in the center of the room so you saw the pieces really well and from all sides. Anyway, Kyle and I were looking for something for my mother. This was when I discovered that my money was gone. Anyway, Mama collects charms, and I wanted to get her one. The clerk was showing me one, and I saw Mason standing by that case, looking all through it. When we were leaving, Mason was gone and I noticed that one of the pieces in the case was missing. It was a small silver carriage thing…."

"It was a napkin holder in the shape of a carriage. I noticed it because my mom would have loved it. She entertains a lot." Kyle sighed. "Neither of us saw Mason take it, but he was by the case, and…." Kyle and Billy both swallowed. "We don't know how he opened it or if he did, but the item was there one minute and gone the next." He turned and glanced around before leaning closer. "Honest. We thought about it all night. Billy and I went back to get the charm for his mom, and there were a bunch of other people in the store. They were looking over the case and stuff. Billy and I bought the charm we'd seen and then left again. But it's pretty obvious that the carriage was gone."

"Did they ask you about it?" Robin questioned.

Billy nodded. "She asked if we'd seen anyone while we were in the store, and we said we weren't sure. Someone might have come in. Neither of us wanted to get Mason in trouble if he didn't do anything."

"But the more we thought about it, the more we think we were wrong." Kyle sat back, his arms folded over his chest, glaring toward the front.

"What if they figure out it was Mason and they think we were in on it?" Billy asked. "Don't places like that have cameras and stuff?"

"You'd think so, but maybe they weren't working. Someone must have had real skill to do that, and they'd likely check that sort of thing." Robin wondered about Mason, but pointedly didn't look at him. "Keep an eye out, and I'll do the same. If he is stealing stuff, then we'll have to catch him at it. Don't mention this to anyone, especially not Mason. I'll talk to Johan so he can watch him too."

Billy and Kyle both nodded and sat back in their seats. Billy took Kyle's hand and leaned against him, more relaxed now that he'd shared his secret. Robin turned in his seat as well and messaged Albert. He recapped what he'd been told and informed him of his course of action.

Albert answered for Robin to be careful and watchful. *If you see anything, call the police. Do not handle it yourself.*

Robin agreed and closed his phone. "We'll be coming into the city soon. Munich has an amazing skyline, but one feature you will not miss is the twin dome towers of the Church of Our Lady. It's a symbol of Munich, and quite unique." Robin cleared his throat and wished he had some more juice with ice. "Johan is going to drive us into the city and drop us off near the Marienplatz. It's the center of town. Have lunch there and then tour the area. The Glockenspiel will chime at three. Our hotel is on the outskirts of the old portion of the city, within walking distance of many of the attractions. Johan will go on to the hotel, and we will walk there together as a group. Is there anyone who feels like they can't make that trip?" Robin did his best not to look directly at Oliver, but kept him in his peripheral vision in case he felt uncomfortable. No one spoke up, which was awesome.

Johan entered city traffic and they made their way to one of the major roundabouts at the edge of the city center. Traffic whizzed around them as Johan opened the bus door, and they all filed off, gathering in a group. Johan got off the bus, opened the small cargo hatch, and pulled out a box for him.

Robin opened it and handed out rainbow hats with the company logo on them. "I thought these might help all of us identify one another. There will be a lot of people, so staying together as a group is important." He pulled his hat out of his bag and put it on. "However, if you do get separated, head to the New Town Hall at three. We will be there for the *Glockenspiel*. It's a guaranteed meeting space."

Johan put the box away and got back on the bus. Robin wished Johan was coming with them, but he had a job to do and so did Robin.

"All right, this way."

ROBIN LED the group down the shopping street to the main pedestrian plaza. "The Marienplatz is the historic center of the city. The old town hall is at the end, and this"—he turned to the gothic-style building with the tower in the center—"is the New Town Hall."

"Is that the Glockenspiel?" Billy asked.

"Yes," Grant answered before Robin could. "It's depicts a famous Bavarian battle and victory." Grant turned away. "I've heard that it's pretty anticlimactic."

Robin had to agree, at least by modern standards. "Think about it. This is a marvel timepiece, and it's hundreds of years old. Every movement is done mechanically with gears and levers. There are no computers and electronics. If you think about it that way, what you're going to see is pretty amazing." He spent some time explaining what the building was, how old it was, and when it was reconstructed. "If you're here for pride weekend, this entire square is packed and the parade goes right through here."

"Will we have time to look around?" Margaret asked.

"Of course." Robin checked his watch. "Go ahead and have some lunch. We'll meet in front of the Glockenspiel at a little before three, watch it chime and move, and then head out to our hotel."

Everyone fanned out in all directions, and Robin found a table at a nearby café and decided to get a light lunch. Surprisingly, he felt lonely. Robin had been here on many tours and usually ended up eating and spending a few hours alone. He'd never minded it before, using the time to settle his thoughts and plan the rest of the tour as well as make arrangements for the next one. But today he was unsettled and kept looking around, hoping Johan would simply appear. Of course, that wasn't going to happen, but he still wished it would.

Robin ordered his lunch and a drink, then sat back as a steady stream of people filed in front of him. He probably should have brought a book or something to pass the time. Still, it gave him some time to—

Robin groaned as Mason pulled out the chair across from him. "What do you want?" Robin asked, letting his annoyance show.

"Everyone else took off, and I saw you here alone." Mason waved, and the server came over. He placed an order, and Robin tried to remember if Mason had always been this rude. Or maybe he'd been blind to the behavior. "You're the only person I really know in this group."

"So why are you so determined to act like an ass?" Robin had had enough of being polite and trying to be professional, letting Mason's behavior run off his back.

"What happened to you?" Mason leaned forward. "You used to be so nice."

"I learned that my boyfriend of five years was a dick of epic proportions, and not in a good way."

Mason flinched.

"You hurt me badly, Mason, and now you expect me to throw open my arms and welcome you back into my life as though nothing happened."

"We should be able to be friends," Mason countered, thanking the server for the drink when he brought it.

"And why is that? Because whatever guy you left me for has skipped away and you're alone?" Robin stopped speaking when the server brought him his lunch. "What if I don't want to be friends, Mason? What if what I want is for you to leave me alone? Are you prepared to do that? Because if you want to be friends, then you need to act like it, and that means respecting my wishes." He sighed softly and picked up his fork. "You always thought what you wanted was good for me, and if it wasn't or if I pushed back, you pressed and badgered me until I gave in." He took a bite of the potatoes. "Sometimes you need to learn how to back off, and you should start now."

Mason turned to the tables around them. "Should I leave?"

"No. The place is packed, so eat your lunch. But give me some space." He ate slowly, feeling better than he had in a while because he'd been able to say his piece to Mason.

"Don't you think it hurts seeing you with him?" Mason asked as he stared at his beer glass.

"Everything isn't about you," Robin answered. "Not to me, not anymore. I've learned something in the last few months, and it's become very clear in the last week. Sometimes things aren't about you, but about the other people around you. I like spending time with Johan."

"You know he'll hurt you," Mason commented. "He'll have to go home after the season, and so will you. Do you think he'll take you home to meet the family?"

Robin shook his head. "He already has. His mom is wonderful, and his family and mine have a lot in common. I don't know what's going to happen between us after the season or after this tour, but a friend would think positively and wish us well, instead of spouting venom and jealousy." Robin returned to his lunch. He refused to rush and allow Mason to think he'd gotten to him.

"We all know the two of you sleep in the same bed every night. The rooms you've been sharing only have one bed. It's pretty common knowledge through the entire tour group."

Robin ignored him. Mason was fishing for something, but Robin wasn't going to let Mason get to him anymore.

He finished his lunch and signaled the waiter. He asked for his bill in German, and when the waiter brought it, Robin paid in cash, thanked him, and got up. "Enjoy your lunch," he told Mason cheerfully, and walked away. Damn, that felt good. There was no need to get angry or upset. Just putting his back to him said more than anything else.

He saw Billy and Kyle wandering through the square. He waved and strode over to join them.

"I didn't get anything yesterday at the Christmas store," Billy said, pointing to a Christmas shop.

"Don't. If we can get moving in the morning, then after we visit the castles tomorrow, we can stop in Oberammergau. It's where they have the Passion Play every ten years. The town is beautiful, and they have a couple of very nice shops that are much less expensive than here in Munich." That reminded him, and Robin pulled out his phone. He messaged Albert to ensure they had ticket reservations and to find out what time they were. Albert messaged back that they were scheduled for eleven and to pick them up at the usual place. Which meant they needed to be moving by eight to ensure they arrived in plenty of time to navigate the town and for everyone to make the ascent up the hill. "We're good for a stop on the way back."

"Awesome," Kyle said, and he and Billy wandered off to meet Grant, Oliver, and Javier.

At a little before three, Robin gathered everyone in the middle of the square.

"Where is Mason?" Billy asked, looking around.

Robin shrugged and shook his head. He wasn't going to try to keep up with him.

The Glockenspiel began running—the knight slayed his opponent, and then the king awarded his laurels. The whole running took less than a minute, and when it was done, the clock chimed the hour.

"That's it." Everyone turned toward him, and Robin saw Mason join the back of the group as though he were trying not to draw anyone's attention. "Let's head this way, and we'll get out of this area. Make sure you have a good hold on everything."

They left the heavily touristy area, and Robin wound them away from the main streets and into more quiet neighborhoods. "I love Munich. It's a city with real charm if you know where to look for it. This is an area of town that was quite affluent. Many of the houses have been converted to apartments or, like the one we're staying in, a hotel." He gathered them all on the sidewalk and pointed. "Just down there a block or so is the Oktoberfest grounds. You can wander through if you'd like to take a look." Robin led the way up to the hotel, where Johan had parked the bus. They went through the process of unloading and getting everyone's room assignments. "Dinner is in the hotel dining room at six thirty."

Robin climbed the stairs with his bag, settled into the chair in the room, and pulled off his shoes and socks to wriggle his toes. He sat back and closed his eyes, then jumped slightly when Johan touched him. He relaxed instantly when Johan gently rubbed first one foot and then another.

"Did you overdo it?"

"No. I was pretty good. And I had things out with Mason." Robin groaned as Johan eased away a day's worth of tension in a few minutes. "Billy and Kyle think Mason is stealing."

"From people in the group?"

"I think he was going to keep Billy's money. He found it on the seat, and I caught him but let him think I didn't realize what he was doing. On the ride here, they told me they thought they might have seen Mason stealing from one of the stores." He relayed what they'd told him. "And today, he snuck up into the group as we were getting ready to leave. I don't know if he's up to something, but he had people to meet in Freiburg. It's all really suspicious."

Johan continued rubbing his feet, and Robin sighed. "That's a pretty huge leap. You were with him for five years. Did you think he was a thief then?"

"No. He traveled for business a few times a year. But he'd always done that for his job. He works for a computer software company, and he had to meet with the various development teams throughout the year." Though Robin started to wonder if those trips weren't the cover for some illicit activities.

"Did you ever go with him?" Johan asked.

"No. They were business trips. He and I went on a few vacations together, usually once a year like most people. He took me to New York and Los Angeles. One year we went to Belgium and Amsterdam. It was fun. But I don't ever remember being suspicious of him. But I am now, and I don't like it." Robin set his feet on the cool floor. "What does it say about me if he was? That I was a clueless idiot for the entire five years we were together?"

"No." Johan placed his hands on Robin's knees and squeezed lightly. "It means that he could be very good at hiding things."

"Albert said to keep an eye on him, and if we see anything, call the police. So that's what I'm going to do." Robin intended to keep a close watch on him as much as he could without letting Mason know he was being watched. "I told Albert you'd help watch him too."

"Of course." Johan stood, and damn it all if he didn't lift Robin right out of the chair and lay him on the bed. Robin would have protested, but Johan rubbed his shoulders and down his arms, and what Robin was going to say died on his lips, replaced with a deep groan. "Just relax for a while and forget about possible criminal exes and everything else. We have an hour and a half until either of us is needed downstairs."

Unless someone needed something and knocked on their door. Barring that, Robin could relax, and he intended to make the very most of the quiet time. It wasn't likely to last forever.

Johan worked his fingers over the top of Robin's chest, leaning over him. Their gazes met, and Robin couldn't look away. He licked his lips and cleared his suddenly dry throat. "I…." Nerves bubbled up from inside as Johan's hands slowly came to a stop and he closed the distance between them, Johan's lips touching his. Heat built like gasoline thrown on a fire, and Robin wound his arms around Johan's neck, kissing him harder, deepening the touch as his body went into overdrive.

Robin arched upward, pressing to Johan, needing to feel himself against Johan. Johan tasted slightly of mint and heat, and all male. Robin tugged on Johan's lips, desperation taking over more quickly than he thought possible. "You've been teasing me for days," he whispered when he pulled back for breath.

"Me? You press that sweet little butt of yours right against me all damn night, and you've been driving me crazy. I want you so much." Johan smiled and kissed him again.

"Well, you drive that bus and I watch you all the time." Robin ran his fingers through Johan's hair. "It's as soft as I dreamed it would be."

"You could have touched anytime," Johan whispered, slipping a little closer.

Robin shook his head. "Sharing a bed is one thing, but sharing touches and being together is quite another. I know it probably doesn't make sense to you, but I didn't feel like I had the right, I guess." He tugged gently, the strands of silken hair sliding along his fingers. "I want you, Johan—you've got to know that by now—but if you don't want me the same way, I understand." It would hurt, yeah. Robin knew that, but… he'd rather have the heartbreak now than once they'd gone too far.

Johan backed away and stood, and Robin figured he had his final answer on the subject. But then Johan tugged his shirt out of his pants and pulled it up over his head, body stretching to his full glory. Acres of golden skin flashed before Robin's eyes. He gasped as Johan sat back down on the side of the bed, pulling at Robin's shirt until they fumbled a little to get it off.

"You say the dumbest things sometimes." Johan wrapped his arms around him and held him chest to chest, guiding their lips together once more.

Robin wasn't going to argue for a second. This was sheer heaven, skin-to-skin contact, heat to flame, kisses that stole his ability to think. The tour group, the entire world—all of it fell away as Johan surrounded him.

"Johan… I just didn't want you to think you had to… you know."

Johan's fingertips traced along his jaw. "I know I don't have to do anything. I want to…. I want you." He pressed Robin back down onto the bed, shifting until he lay right next to him. He drew Robin to him like a moth to flame, and no matter what, there was no way Robin was going to turn away. His entire body thrummed with excitement, blood racing through him, and for a split second, he wondered if the excitement and anticipation would be too much for him. Johan backed away, gentling his kisses, running his hands slowly up and over Robin's chest.

Robin stilled for a second. Someone touching his scars always sent a weird sensation racing through him. Robin waited for that to happen, but it didn't, not this time. All he felt was Johan's touch and the heat that radiated from him with every movement. He tugged Johan down once again and kissed him hard, giving himself over.

Johan's fingers worked open his belt and then the top of his pants. Robin held his breath, pulling in his belly as the pressure around his waist eased and the fabric parted.

"Johan…," Robin breathed, and he stopped.

"I love the way you say my name. Please do it again." Johan slipped his hand inside Robin's briefs, and Robin breathed his name again as Johan cupped him, rubbing his finger down the ridge of his cock. A flood of near ecstasy washed over him, and he groaned softly.

Johan worked his pants and underwear down, and Robin shifted his legs until they fell away. He was naked, bared completely to Johan. He knew Johan had seen him in the sauna, but to be completely naked in front of him was both nerve-inducing and exciting at the same time. "You're beautiful," Johan whispered, his breath ghosting over Robin's lips.

Robin rocked his head on the pillow.

"Don't you have a saying about beauty being in the eye of the seer?" Johan blinked, his deep brown eyes shining in the light coming in from the window.

"Yes."

"Then don't argue. I know what I see and what I want." Johan kissed him again. "I want you to stay here with me. Lead more tours, and I will be your driver during the day and your lover at night." He kissed Robin before he could answer, and Robin returned it. He wasn't sure if that was possible, but now was not the time to pop Johan's bubble with logic and practicalities. Sometimes it was nice just to be asked, no matter what the answer might have to be.

Robin worked open Johan's belt, his fingers fumbling in his haste. He needed to feel him against him. Johan sighed softly and got off the bed once again, this time to strip off the rest of his clothes.

He stood naked near the side of the bed in all his glory, a masculine feast for Robin's eyes only, standing tall, cock thrusting toward the ceiling. Robin groaned and slowly reached out to close his fingers around Johan's length, drawing Johan forward, heat radiating from Johan to him. Robin needed all he could get.

Johan slowly climbed back onto the bed and pulled the two of them together, heat melding and desire building in seconds. "I don't want to squish you," Johan whispered as Robin tugged him down, reveling in Johan's weight and solidity on top of him.

"I'm not made of glass," Robin whispered, then kissed away Johan's protest, slipping his tongue between Johan's luscious lips. He groaned as the intensity built, Johan's cock sliding along his, the kisses deepening along with desire that swelled enough to fill the room.

Johan slid his lips down Robin's neck, and Robin groaned and stretched, giving Johan better access. He continued lower, sucking lightly on Robin's nipples and then using his lips and tongue to blaze a trail of heat down his belly. Robin's muscles fluttered with anticipation. He closed his eyes again, running his fingers through Johan's hair, which fell onto his skin, tickling and teasing at the same damned time. He willed Johan to go further, biting his lower lip to keep from screaming out what he wanted. When Johan blew his hot breath over his length, Robin tensed, and he gasped loudly when Johan's lips closed over him for the first time.

It took all his willpower not to thrust forward to bury himself inside Johan's throat. He wanted it more than anything, but he held still and let Johan set the pace. And one hell of a pace it was. He groaned even louder as Johan took more and more of him into his wet heat. Needing to see, Robin opened his eyes and lifted his head, nearly coming at the sight of his cock disappearing into Johan's talented mouth.

Johan pulled away, their gazes meeting, and then Johan kissed him hard. Robin tasted some of himself on Johan's tongue, sucking it as Johan closed his arms around him. He wanted to reciprocate, but Johan held him too tightly, kissing him deeply as his hips thrust back and forth. Robin's cock slid along Johan's heaving belly, and pressure built to the point he had little control over his own body. Robin's need took over, instinct propelling him until heat splashed between them, sending Robin over the edge.

He held still, gasping for air, as waves of ecstasy washed over him. Damn, he loved that floaty-cloud feeling. Johan didn't move either, holding him until his eyes drooped downward. Then Johan's weight lifted. He left the room and returned with a towel. Robin intended to protest that he could clean himself up, but Johan was so gentle and caring that he kept his eyes closed and waited for Johan to rejoin him. Without much effort, Robin slipped into a doze, holding Johan in his arms.

"HOW MUCH longer before we get there?" Javier asked the following morning as they rode to Neuschwanstein. Robin swore the man acted worse than a six-year-old.

"Half an hour or so," Oliver answered, and Javier turned to look out the window. Oliver rolled his eyes and sat back, watching Javier.

They were slightly ahead of schedule, and when they pulled into Füssen, Johan parked the bus and everyone stood.

"Please remain in your seats for a few more minutes," Robin instructed. "I need to get the tickets."

He hurried off the bus and went up to the ticket window. He gave them the name of the tour group, and they handed him the reserved tickets with their time stamp. The town was already busy, and there was a line forming at the window and a steady stream of people heading up the hill. Thankfully Albert was smart enough not to get him a ticket. Robin had made the trip once before, and it had nearly worn him out completely. The road was uphill the entire way. There were carriages that would take you up part of the way, but that was all.

Robin returned to the bus. "Okay. Please file off, and I'll give you each a ticket. As you can see, there is a time stamp, and you have a little less than an hour to get to the top of the hill. Don't wait down here. I suggest you go right up. There will be lines that form for your ticket time and a board to explain where to go."

Everyone seemed to heed his advice and headed uphill, which meant he had a couple of hours to kill at least.

"You can go if you like," Robin offered, smiling at Johan.

"No. I'm fine right here. It's so busy that I need to stay with the bus. Sometimes they ask us to move." He stayed in his seat, leaning slightly over the steering wheel. "Don't you go?"

"Not anymore." Robin looked away sheepishly. "I didn't get as much sleep last night as I usually do." A smile formed on his face without the least bit of help from him. "Do you have to stay in the bus or…?"

"No. I'll put my number on the door and they will call. Why?"

"We could get some coffee or something," Robin offered. "When they get back, we can let the group have lunch here and then make a shopping stop. We'll have plenty of time."

"Sure." Johan locked up the bus and put his sign where it would be seen. Then they went into the restaurant and took a table where they could look out at the passing crowds. "I went on a tour of the castle earlier this year and was disappointed. They used to give personalized tours, but now it's all electronic."

"Yeah, and I hate to say it, but the place is looking shabby and showing a lot of wear. I suppose millions of people traipsing through it for decades will do that.

Still, if we didn't come, every group would ask why, so Albert includes it on the tour."

They ordered a drink and some light pastries and sat watching the hordes of people descend on the small town.

"You asked me something last night," Robin said. "I think I need to give you an answer."

"Yes," Johan agreed. "But you do not owe me an answer. Not right now. I know what I want, but I have to give you a chance to want what I want." He grinned, and it took Robin a second to figure out what Johan was saying. "This is new for you and—"

Robin huffed softly. "Why do you have to be so danged perfect all the time?" he asked with mock exasperation. "I'm a bundle of leftover teenage angst, and you seem to know what I need. It isn't fair. You're *too* damned perfect." He sipped his juice and turned to watch the ever-growing crowds of people headed up the hill. It was a steady stream in one direction that eventually would become two-way traffic.

Johan leaned over the table "I'm not perfect. Just ask my mother. She will tell you that I'm stubborn, and most of the time, I do not know when to quit. I know what I want, and I'm willing to be patient. My mom would also tell you that I waste my life… at least if she knew you better." Johan turned away. "I went to university." He shivered. "In Germany we take tests, and those who do well go to university. Those who do not go to other schools. It is how it is. Very little choice built into the system. We all know this since we are small."

Robin knew of the system, and he would have loved to have been able to take advantage of a free education. Instead, he'd had to work for it. Especially after all the homeschooling. His mother…. Robin pulled his thoughts back to where they belonged. “What was so bad?”

“My mother and father were very proud. They want me to study business so I can help run the restaurant. I wanted….” He groaned. “I like working with my hands. I make things.” He pulled out his phone and brought up his photo gallery. “I make these.”

There were pictures of wooden toys that looked somewhat like the ones in the tourist shops, except finer and with more details. Then there were tables that looked amazing—like old, traditional Black Forest work, absolutely stunning.

“I did what they want and then turned away. My parents were not happy. They wanted more for me, and they are ashamed for a long time that I drive a bus.” He shrugged. “I just wanted to be happy.” He lowered his voice. “My mama convinced me to quit. She said I should do more with my life, and I was about to.” Johan nodded and smiled. “Then I drove for you. And I thought you were really cute and funny sometimes with the groups. They like you. But you did not see me. Just the hair.” He made a face, and Robin closed his eyes, wishing he could take back what had happened before. It hadn’t been fair. He hadn’t given Johan a chance at all, just let appearances dictate his opinion.

“Why did you do that? I was pretty nasty to you, but you asked to be my driver again? Hell, you planned a lot of what’s happened on this tour. I don’t understand why.”

“Because you were so nice to everyone else, and I thought I might have scared you.” Johan nodded and groaned softly. “My mother hated my beard and the long hair. She told me that if I wanted people to see me, then I needed to give them something pleasant to look at.” Johan grinned. “Mama is practical and funny sometimes. I cut off my beard and cut my hair. Mama wanted it shorter."

"No," Robin said quickly. "I like your hair. It's beautiful the way it cascades to your shoulders." His mind went to the night before and how he had run his fingers through it over and over. Maybe he was starting to develop some kind of hair kink… at least for Johan's.

"I felt better once the beard was gone, and Mama was happy too. I thought I looked better, and when I saw you again, I knew you noticed me." Johan chuckled. "You blushed when I watched you. I saw you turn red, and I know you saw me then."

"Yeah, but I should have seen you before. I was… intimidated, I guess." Robin wasn't sure how he could explain all of why that was. "My mom had a brother-in-law. He's dead now, thank goodness. I hope he rots in hell forever." Robin wished he drank, because he needed one about now. "I was weak some of the time—I told you that. After the second surgery to fix my heart, I felt better for a few years, and I could go out and be a lot more normal. My aunt and uncle lived in Florida, about fifty miles from Disney. Aunt Gladys is Mama's sister, and she invited me to come stay with them for a week in the fall. I was fourteen, and Mama put me on a plane and Aunt Gladys was there to meet me. I thought it was going to be fun and we'd get to do stuff." Robin shook his head. "Uncle Frank was a huge bear of a man, and he had a long beard like some mountain man on television. He and Aunt Gladys fought the entire time I was there because he didn't want me there and she had invited me. He refused to have any of *his money* used to take me anywhere. I ended up watching television for a week and then going home, and when I asked to go to Disney, like any kid would, he yelled at me and said I was too weak to enjoy it anyway. He even called me names to Aunt Gladys. I really hated him. Aunt Gladys left him a while after that, and he died of cancer. At least that's what Mom told me. All I can say is that I hope it was painful." Robin grew agitated and clenched his hands into fists just thinking about it.

"Did you see him again before he died?" Johan asked.

"Once. He came to Milwaukee for Christmas—I guess it was just before Aunt Gladys kicked his butt to the curb. The two of them visited, and Mama asked me to go to my room. Then she laid into him.... My mama is generally soft-spoken, but she said things that turned the air blue. I think she might have hit him, and then she threw him out of the house, saying that her sister was welcome anytime, but he could go sit at the curb with the rest of the trash." Robin smiled a little. "The next year I got sick again. Mama had said that she would take me to Disney, but it never happened." He shrugged. He groaned softly and got his mind back on his original train of thought. "I know it's no excuse, but I might have flashed on some of my residual feelings for my awful uncle and took them out on you. I don't really know." He turned to watch people once more, the restaurant filling behind him, getting a little louder.

"Mason...," Johan said, pointing across the way.

"What's he doing back so quickly?" Robin asked, checking the time. The group should be in the castle for their tour. There was no way he should be at the bottom of the hill. He stood near a lamppost, his pack on his back, looking from side to side. Come to think of it, Mason had brought his pack with him, which was odd, because they wouldn't allow him to enter with it. Robin excused himself, telling Johan he'd be right back, and left the restaurant.

As he stepped out onto the sidewalk, a man approached Mason. He stopped, spoke quickly to Mason, and they walked back toward where the buses were parked. Robin tried to follow but couldn't see them. He glanced around and returned to the restaurant.

"I don't know what's going on." Robin's curiosity was definitely piqued, and he was going to find out what was happening on his tour. Any trust he had for Mason was long gone.

Ten minutes later Mason came back into view.

"Look, his pack is empty. It was full before, and now it's hanging there and flat." Robin leaned closer to the window. "What the hell is he doing?" When Mason looked toward them, he turned away and lifted his glass to his lips, hoping he'd covered the fact that he'd been watching.

"This isn't good," Johan said.

Robin agreed, but he had nothing other than suspicions and supposition. "But I don't know what to do."

"Nothing to do. If he's a thief, then confronting him could put you in danger."

Robin nodded. What Johan said made a lot of sense, and it was probably best that he stayed out of it. He finished his drink and ate the last bite of pastry, trying to put Mason out of his mind.

A few minutes later, Oliver and Javier exited the path from the hill, with Oliver looking very pale, a hand over his chest.

"We have to go." Robin pulled out his wallet and handed some money to their server, then practically pulled Johan along with him. He raced over to where

Oliver sat on the grass beside the path, as pale as a ghost and gasping for air. "What happened?"

"I'm okay," Oliver wheezed. Robin wasn't so sure and pulled out his phone to call for help. Oliver shook his head as he held Robin's hand. "I overdid it. That's all." He raised his gaze, and Javier sat down next to him, taking Oliver's hand and putting an arm around his shoulders.

"Do you want some water?" Javier asked, and before Oliver could answer, Johan had hurried away.

"I should have taken the carriage ride up and not tried to walk the whole way." Oliver leaned on Javier, who held him.

"Then why did you?" Javier asked with surprising gentleness.

"I didn't want you to be disappointed," Oliver said, and Javier clicked his teeth and held Oliver closer. "I'm getting old, I know that, and…." Oliver closed his eyes as his breathing returned to normal. "You're going to leave me behind, and I need to figure out how to keep up."

Johan returned and handed Oliver a bottle of water. He drank and seemed much better.

Robin took Johan's arm, and they left the two of them alone. Robin would watch that Oliver was okay, but he and Javier seemed to need some time alone.

"Wow," Johan said as they found an empty bench. "I thought they…."

Robin understood immediately. "I know. With all their bickering and Javier's impatience, I thought he didn't care for Oliver particularly." Javier still held Oliver, helping him to his feet. Robin motioned and stood to give them room on the bench.

"I'm sorry," Oliver apologized again. "I just overdid it." He sat with a sigh.

"When we get you home, you're going to the doctor, and he's going to give you a thorough physical. You haven't been in a long time, and you need to take better care of yourself." The concern was genuine and nice to hear. "Maybe we'll find a trainer who can help you get stronger if that's what you want. We can go to the gym together." Javier truly seemed shaken. "Whatever you need, we'll see to it that you get." Once again Javier sat and held Oliver closer.

"The food is good in the restaurant. Why don't you get out of the sun and have a little something to eat? Oliver can relax until it's time to go on." Robin saw them inside and caught the others as they came down the hill to tell them to eat and that they would leave at one thirty as planned.

"Have you ever gone up to that one?" Billy asked, pointing to the yellow castle on the hill.

"That's Hohenschwangau, and no. Usually there isn't time. Someday maybe. That's one of the castles that's still owned by the family. It isn't fanciful the way the other one is. Though it is where Ludwig spent part of his childhood. There are books in the gift shops with pictures of it, I'm sure." Robin could remember seeing them the last time he looked around.

"We should eat," Kyle said gently, and led Billy inside.

"Did you have a good time?" Robin asked Lily and Margaret as they came down the hill.

"Not quite what I was expecting. It's fake, like some movie set," Lily commented. But they were both smiling, and Lily seemed happy and much less stressed than she'd been when the tour started.

"That it is. Now, later in the tour when we go to Trier, we're taking a trip to another castle that's just the opposite. It's very much real, and it's been in the same family for almost nine hundred years. It's one of the highlights of the tour for me."

Lily leaned close as if to share a secret. "There was a man on the same tour with us who kept looking at me."

"And she was such a trollop and flirted back," Margaret teased, and both of them giggled softly.

"It's good to know I've still got it, even if I am rusty." Lily motioned to Grant, and he followed them inside for lunch.

"This tour seems to have been good for a lot of them." Johan nudged Robin slightly.

"Vacations are good for people."

Johan sighed. "You do not see it. You listened to Lily and helped her. You did the same with Billy and helped him find his money. He found the courage to tell Kyle, and they are happy. You helped Oliver, and look at him and Javier. They are like turtledoves now. The others are happy and having a good time. Only Mason is still grumpy, but the others ignore him." Johan seemed pleased. "You do a good job, and you deserve to be happy too."

"I only did my job," Robin protested. "And they wanted to be happy—they just needed some time without the stress of everyday life to see it."

"Even Grant is happier," Johan said, turning. Robin followed his gaze to where Grant sat with all the ladies, laughing and smiling brightly. "You did that. And this tour isn't unique. You did it on the first tour I was with you too. Remember Jerry and Martin? They complained about everything for three whole days. I thought about locking them off the bus. They got on my nerves. Then all of a sudden they were making goo-goo eyes at each other for the rest of the trip."

Robin laughed. He couldn't help it.

"You did something," Johan challenged.

"That night at dinner, I asked them how they'd met, and they told me their story from many years before. Jerry had been in the Marines, and Martin designed men's clothes. Jerry was engaged, and his wife-to-be wanted him to get some stylish clothes and recommended Martin. Apparently Martin knew the instant they met that Jerry was going to be his and made his intentions known. They danced around each other for weeks until Martin simply cornered Jerry in the dressing room and 'kissed the life out of him'—Jerry's words exactly. The engagement didn't last much longer after that." Robin smiled. "Those two told the story in fits and starts, finishing each other's sentences, and after that, they were…."

"They remembered what they loved about each other," Johan supplied.

"I think so. They were much happier, anyway, and had a lot of fun." Robin sighed. "I got a card from Martin last week. It was waiting for me when I got home from my last tour. They'd had the time of their lives and were both so grateful for the talk and the happy times." He forced a smile and failed miserably. "There was also a newspaper clipping in the envelope." Robin blinked, turning to Johan, burying his face in his shoulder. "It was Jerry's obituary. From the date, he died the week after they got home." He tried to hold himself together and faltered. "Written in the margin was a note that read: 'Thank you. He passed away happy, and our last memories together are joyous ones.'"

Johan put an arm around him and stayed quiet, holding him as they sat on the bench with what seemed like the rest of the tourist world passing by in front of them, but Robin felt safe in the bubble that Johan created around them.

"I'm afraid of dying," Robin admitted around his sore throat. "I used to think about what it would be like, but I don't want to do it. Sometimes I wake up at night and think I see the damned Grim Reaper at the foot of the bed, waiting for me. And… I want to go like Jerry. I want to be happy. But then I wonder what it must be like for Martin to be left behind. He and Jerry had been together for over thirty years, and then he was gone."

"But they had all that time together."

Robin wiped his eyes and sniffled, pulling away. "Yes. And I'll never have that, and neither will anyone I let in my life." He took a deep breath. "I'm already on borrowed time from someone who died prematurely, and what will happen when that time is up?" Robin hated that they were back to this again, but facts were facts, and there was nothing Robin could do to change them.

Johan shook his head. "Do you think about dying all the time and what will happen?"

Robin swallowed. "Sometimes. I've already come face-to-face with death and survived. I'm sure you saw *Meet Joe Black* when death decides to see what it's like to be human? I've met him too. He paid me a visit, and I can tell you he didn't look anything like Brad Pitt. And he's pissed because he thought he had me." Robin smiled to make light of what he was saying. "Anyway, I know I'm not going to get another chance at love."

Johan stood, and Robin figured he'd finally scared him away. Maybe deep down that's what he'd wanted all along. He wasn't really sure.

"You're a real pain in the ass, and you watch too many movies." He tugged Robin to his feet. "Death isn't following you, because he doesn't have to. He always gets everyone in the end, so he is patient. And I think, if you watch that Brad Pitt movie, that even death wants to have a good time every now and then, so why shouldn't the rest of us?"

"Where are we going?" Robin asked.

"Well, you and I are having lunch with the others, and then I'm driving you to this shopping stop, and from there we're going to have more fun. This is their vacation, and if you ask me, you should be more concerned with living than dying."

Robin hadn't asked him, but Johan was right. It was part of why he'd come here in the first place.

Johan led him across the street to a place with window service and returned with two paper boats. "Currywurst," he said when he set them down. "Germany's answer to the hot dog." He grinned, and they ate.

"You remembered how much I love this," Robin said as he took a bite, the curry ketchup tingling on his tongue.

"Who doesn't?" Johan asked.

Robin noticed Mason a few yards away, standing alone, and groaned to himself, tilting his head for him to join them. Mason was a shit and he was always going to be a shit, but holding on to the anger and resentment wasn't going to help Robin. And in less than a week, he was never going to see him again. Besides, keeping him close was an easy way to keep an eye on him.

CHAPTER 6

"GOOD MORNING," Robin said once they were underway two days later. "I really hope you enjoyed Munich and got to see all the things you wanted to."

It hadn't been on the official schedule, but on their last free day, Robin had led a small group to the Alte Pinakothek art museum. They had gone by subway, which was an experience for all of them.

"We're going to be on the bus for a while this morning, which is why we left a little early. We will be heading out of Bavaria and into the Mosel region. This is one of the great wine valleys of Germany, and many of the great grapes of the area were brought here by the Romans two thousand years ago."

"Will there be Roman ruins?" Oliver asked.

"Yes. The Black Gate is very important in Trier, where we're headed," Grant answered and turned back forward, reddening as Lily and Margaret flashed him a sly look from across the aisle.

"Yes. The Porta Nigra, or Black Gate, is a large Roman-era structure in Trier. There are also the ruins of an arena, a full bath complex, and many others. Trier was founded as a Roman city, and there are plenty of reminders of that history. We will be there two nights. Today Johan and I will guide you on a bus tour around the city, and you'll be able to explore the ruins. Tomorrow afternoon we'll be driving to the small hamlet of Moselkern so you can visit Burg Eltz. There will be time to explore on your own as well, so sit back, relax, and close your eyes if you want. If you have any questions, please feel free to ask. I will be glad to answer them." Robin waited, but even Grant seemed tired and closed his eyes. They had been touring for over a week, and everyone had been going almost nonstop, with plenty of walking, shopping, and sights to see, so a few hours on the bus wasn't necessarily a bad thing.

Johan motioned with his head before Robin took his seat. He leaned down so they could speak quietly. "Did you see Mason's pack when he boarded the bus? It was full again… and heavy."

Robin nodded. "I know. I'm going to have to watch him and see where he goes."

"Or keep him really busy," Johan offered.

Robin wasn't sure he liked that particular suggestion. After the last two days of fun during the day and even more intimate fun at night with Johan, the thought of spending time with Mason in any way was unappealing at best.

"I mean, I know Trier pretty well. I'll add a few stops to the sightseeing tour, and with lunch, it should keep all of them, Mason included, very busy for much of the day."

"Not bad. It will throw off the timetable a little," Robin said, but maybe that wasn't such a bad thing. If Mason was up to something, a little spontaneity could chuck a wrench in the works.

Robin sat back down, half watching Johan as he drove, and composed an email to his mother. He figured that would be the easiest way to tell her all about Johan. Not that Robin could quite figure things out yet. He thought maybe his mother would have some insight—at least he hoped so.

He set his phone aside, leaving the message in his drafts. Maybe he needed to call and talk to her. Sometimes the seven-hour time difference sucked, because he really could use her advice about now. He and Albert sometimes talked about personal stuff, but this was a little heavy for him to talk to Albert about. They joked and kidded, but serious topics weren't their thing.

Robin sat back and closed his eyes, sighing gently as his thoughts whirled in circles. Yes, he wanted to see where things went with Johan. He still had four more tours booked before the season was over, so he was planning to be in Germany for nearly two months yet. But was it fair to continue when he was eventually going back home? Or did he want to go back at all? Robin scowled at the thought of his mother and how she'd completely slip a gasket if he told her that. His mom would be fine with whatever he decided in the end, but the process of getting her acceptance could be painful… for both of them, especially if he sprang something like that on her. Not that Robin could blame her. His mother had worried, fussed, and fought for him since Robin was born. She couldn't just turn that sort of protective instinct off. That was part of what he needed to talk to her about.

Robin rested, staring at the back of Johan's head, wisps of Johan's black hair touching the seat. God, he wanted to touch it, run his fingers along the silky strands. It was so easy to picture himself back in the hotel room, with Johan next to him, Robin's eyes closed and Johan's fingers wandering over his ever-heating skin, inhaling Johan's scent with every breath until he was seconds from exploding. He could live like that forever and be happy. Robin knew it. And Johan wouldn't hurt him—something deep in his soul told him Johan would treasure him. But what could Robin ever give him in return?

Someone sat in the seat next to him, and Robin startled out of his thoughts.

"I never got a chance to thank you properly for your help the other day," Oliver said softly. "Sometimes I still think I'm a lot younger than I really am. Or maybe sometimes I wish I could turn the clock backward." He turned around, and Robin followed his gaze to a sleeping Javier. "I never expected he'd want to be with me." Oliver turned back around. "I thought he was only after my money, so I took things slow. Then he started to bicker and argue with me." He shook his head. "If he'd been after my money, he'd have gone along with everything I said and he'd have done anything to make me happy. He didn't. He was himself. The pain in the butt." Oliver smiled. "Sometimes you young kids don't know a good thing until it's gone or you've wrung all the fun out of it."

Robin wasn't quite sure how to take that at all. "Oliver, I—"

Oliver plowed on. "I saw you at the spa, so I know you've had some health issues in your life. So have I. They were part of the reason I went out with Javier. I thought I was going to die after I had a heart attack at fifty-one. And that kind of brush leaves a mark on a person's soul. I know it did on me, and I see that in you sometimes." He met Robin's gaze in all seriousness. "Javier started out as a midlife crisis, but I'm happy for the most part—probably more so than I deserve, if I'm honest."

"I don't understand what you're trying to tell me," Robin said, his discomfort rising a little.

"We have all seen the way you and Johan look at each other. Some people were even taking bets on when something would happen between you two. For a couple days there, the eye-fucking was steaming up the bus windows." Oliver chuckled. "It still does sometimes." He winked, and Robin rolled his eyes, saying nothing. He was neither going to confirm or deny.

"What are you getting at?" Robin asked, feeling a little annoyed.

"Nothing bad at all. It's just that you seem to be… 'holding back' is the phrase I'd use, I guess." Oliver looked at Johan, who glanced over at them and then back at the road. "I'll tell you this. You get one chance at life, be it long or short, and you should make the most of it, no matter what. When our time comes, we all have regrets, but I don't want to look back and say that I gave up on a chance for love. And you shouldn't either. I hope I have thirty years left, but who knows? I can tell you that there are things I wish I'd done differently when I was your age. I played it safe, when now I know that if I'd taken chances…." He shrugged. "Or one chance in particular. At the end, you regret what you didn't do a hell of a lot more than the things you did." Oliver squeezed his hand and then stood and made his way back to Javier.

Oliver was probably right. If Johan was willing to take the chance on him, who was he to tell him no? Robin just had to make sure Johan understood everything that was possible and then let him truly decide what he wanted. If Robin was lucky—damn lucky—after all that, Johan would still be interested.

Robin sat back, having made a decision he could be happy with, smiling to himself as the scenery outside the window changed to valleys and long stretches of river with the sun sparkling on the water.

"ALL RIGHT, everyone, welcome to Trier," Robin said as they entered the city, the people on the bus perking up after the quiet ride. "Johan is going to take us by the major sights and to the Roman-era basilica. We'll make a few stops so you can get out to take pictures." Robin turned to Johan. "I know you know the city better than I do. Let's go to the bath ruins, amphitheater, and the Black Gate in whatever order works with traffic. We can also go to the river. Afterward, there's the pedestrian zone." He turned back to the others. "All right, there is one other thing I want to caution everyone about. One of the things you will see a lot of in town is various Roman coins for sale. Be skeptical of everything. Many of them are real, but the price is five to six times what you could get an authentic coin for on eBay or at a dealer back home. This is a touristy area."

Johan drove them to the Porta Nigra first—a large, imposing stone structure, as black as coal, all that was left of the Roman fortifications. Johan parked, and everyone got off the bus to take pictures and wander a little, stretching their legs.

"I love it here," Johan said as Robin waited with him on the bus, watching everyone mill about. "I live every day with my own history staring me in the face. We get used to it. But this always makes me think. One of my ancestors probably fought the Romans two thousand years ago."

"You could be part Roman," Robin offered with a grin. "I think I can see you that way, dressed like one of those statues with nothing but a cloth around your waist and a helmet, carrying a sword." He leaned closer. "Though you have a really nice sword of your own."

Johan snorted. "Is that your version of talking dirty?" He got out of his seat and took the one next to Robin. Robin wasn't sure of he should be offended or not. "We'll work on it. Trust me."

The change in subject nearly gave him whiplash. "Okay. You got off topic."

"I think it was you who got us off topic." Johan bumped him with his shoulder. "I was saying that this helps remind me just how far back my history goes. It's rather humbling."

"And exciting." Robin rested his head on Johan's shoulders for a few minutes, until it was nearly time for everyone to return.

Johan returned to his seat and opened the door, letting everyone file back on.

The ruins of the baths were impressive, but they were mostly just walls of stone and brick—ruins that left a lot to the imagination. The amphitheater was largely made using an impression in the ground that had been shaped and built into the bowl-shaped hillsides. The floor had been restored, so visiting gave a real sense of what the arena had been like. A tour was about to start, so most of the group joined it. It meant some additional time, but Robin was happy they were enjoying themselves.

"How much longer are we going to be?" Mason asked when he boarded the bus first, dropping onto his seat.

"Why?" Robin turned around. "You have a pressing appointment or something?" Mason flinched, but Robin pretended not to see. "We're going to stop for lunch and some shopping in the pedestrian zone, and then go to the river. We'll get to the hotel a little later than planned." He turned back around and waited for the others to climb back on the bus.

The pedestrian zone was filled with restaurants and shops. Robin loved the town's winding streets, which dated back to the Romans. Johan had to stay with the bus, so Robin was on his own. It seemed strange not to have Johan with him. Robin found an Italian restaurant and took a table on the sidewalk under an umbrella.

A server handed him a menu. Robin wasn't super hungry, but the pesto sounded good. He sat and waited for the food to arrive, wishing he had someone to sit with.

"Are you alone?" a man asked in perfect American English.

Robin waved to the other chair, and the young man, probably a student judging from the old backpack he had slung over his back, sat down. "Robin."

"Spencer." He smiled and set his pack next to his chair. "I'm on my study year abroad and wanted to take some time to see the country before I started classes in a month or so."

Robin remembered his college years, but he hadn't gotten to study abroad because of his health. Thankfully his family spoke German, and he had plenty of people to practice on. "I'm a tour guide." He smiled. "I'm leading a group of tourists through the country, and today they have lunch on their own, so I have some time to myself."

"How much time?" Spencer grinned a bright, full smile, his eyes catching the light as he leaned forward. "You're really cute…."

Robin chuckled. "Thank you. But I have a sort-of boyfriend, and, well…." Damn, it was nice to be flirted with like that. Hell, it was a definite come-on, and that was ego-boosting. Heat spread from deep inside, a fluttering excitement that Robin hadn't felt before—not for the man sitting across the table, but for the one back at the bus, waiting for him. "I have to have lunch and then get back to my group."

Spencer shrugged. "Dang it, I had to take a shot." He sat back, and the server took his order when she returned with Robin's drink.

They made small talk as they ate. The lunch was comfortable and nice, with little continuing innuendo, though Robin got the idea that Spencer was hoping he'd change his mind. That wasn't going to happen. After they paid their bills, Robin said goodbye and walked back in the direction of the bus, smiling to himself.

"Who was the cutie?" Mason quizzed as he approached Robin.

"Spencer? Just a stranger who shared my table." Robin turned away from Mason and continued on his way. Who he had lunch with was none of his business anyway.

"It didn't look that way from what I saw," Mason pressed, and Robin paused.

"The tables were full, so he asked if he could sit down. It's what Europeans do, and accepting someone else at the table was nice. I didn't sit alone, and we had a nice conversation." He shook his head. "Only you would make someone sitting down with me seem dirty and unseemly." Robin noticed that Mason's pack seemed a lot lighter again. It had been full that morning. "Why don't you mind your own business?" He stepped closer. "I don't think you'd want me or Johan taking a huge interest in yours."

Mason flinched.

"Don't be late. You don't want to get left." Robin had to take the dig at him because it was too good to resist, and not turning to see his reaction was the best satisfaction of all. Mason needed to get the hell out of his life once and for all. Robin was ready to move on, and his ex being around had been a millstone around his neck for days, but that weight was gone. Robin owed Mason nothing at all and didn't give a damn what he thought or how he reacted about anything. Mason was his past. His future, or what he hoped might be his future, waited for him back at the bus.

Robin stopped at a stand on the way back and got some sausage rolls for Johan, then carried them back to the bus and handed Johan the to-go bag. He pulled a bottle of water from his messenger bag and handed that to him as well.

"That damn pack of his is emptying once again," Robin reported. He leaned down to kiss Johan and then sat right behind him. "We need to find out what the hell is going on." He didn't care what Albert or anyone said. If Mason was up to something illegal, they needed to know and put a stop to it.

"There have been people watching the bus," Johan explained, turning toward him, eating the sausage roll with a grin. "They're trying not to be obvious about it, but the men at the edge of the yard have been smoking and talking for nearly an hour, and one of them keeps watching, I can feel it." Johan was clearly on edge, and Robin placed his hands on his shoulders, rubbing gently as Johan continued eating.

"I don't like this at all." Robin's own anxiety shot upward. "And I hate that he's on the tour. The guy is a real weasel, and I can't figure out why I didn't see it before." He really should have. Robin grew quiet, rubbing Johan's shoulders, the contact reassuring him while Johan continued eating.

"We need to play dumb and not let on that we know anything about him. We can still watch, and maybe we will have a chance to look through that pack while he's busy." Johan smiled, tugging Robin down for a kiss. He tasted like the spice from the sausage and the butter in the roll. "If those men are watching the bus, let's give them something to look at." He kissed Robin hard, sending a wave of desire running through him, his skin heating and his pulse running faster.

Robin pulled back a little. "A college student ate lunch with me." He swallowed. "The café was full and I was alone, so Spencer asked if he could sit with me. He was younger and nice, and…." Robin bit his lower lip. "He made a pass at me." Damn it all, he could feel his cheeks heating. "I told him no, that I had a sort-of boyfriend…." God, he hoped Johan understood what he was trying to say.

"Sort-of boyfriend?" Johan asked, his eyes darkening.

"Well, I didn't know what we were, but I wanted him to know that I wasn't free and had no intention of going off with him." Robin stammered a little.

"That you think of me as your sort-of boyfriend? You think that would be okay with me?" Johan asked, and Robin sighed as he realized Johan was teasing him.

"Don't be mean to me," Robin countered, and Johan chuckled.

"How about we say that, yes, you are my boyfriend. That way there is none of this 'sort-of' about it." He kissed Robin once again, then ate the last of his lunch and put the bag and the empty water bottle in the trash.

"Okay…," Robin said. "Mason saw me with Spencer and was being nasty about it. I told him that he wouldn't like it if I stuck my nose in his business. He paled instantly. I turned away as though the line was a throwaway, but I think I might have made him a little nervous."

Johan mused a minute. "That may be good. Let him be nervous and on edge. We will watch."

A knock on the bus door had Robin pulling away. Oliver and Javier climbed on when Johan opened it. The others returned as well, with Mason bringing up the rear. His backpack appeared the same as the last time Robin had seen him.

Robin avoided eye contact with Mason and got to work. "I hope you all had a good lunch." He smiled as they settled in their seats and Johan pulled out of his parking space. "I have a few interesting facts for you. The Porta Nigra contains no mortar. The blocks are held together with iron pegs, which is pretty cool. Right now, we are heading to the Basilica of Constantine. It's also of Roman origin and is one of the largest expanses from that era still under roof. It's a wonderful place to look around and get some pictures. I'd like to take one of our entire group there." He held on to the back of a seat, standing so everyone could hear. "Does anyone have any questions?"

"What are we doing after this?" Billy asked as he rummaged through his pack.

"Tomorrow we will travel up the Mosel River to visit the best-preserved medieval castle in Europe. Burg Eltz is all original and is still in the family, as it has been for nearly nine hundred years. It's one of my favorite places to visit. There's armor and weapons, as well as original kitchen wares and all the things of daily life. The following day we will travel to the Rhine. Instead of the bus, we'll take a boat south." Robin smiled. "The Rhine flows north, so we'll be going against the current, and there are a ton of castles along the way. It's a wonderful, relaxing day on the water."

"What if the weather is bad?" Lily asked.

"The boat has an interior, so if it rains, you can sit inside and watch through the windows," Robin answered.

"It's supposed to be nice," Grant said quietly, and Robin relayed the information.

"Are there any other questions I can answer for you?" Robin asked.

"Yes," Mason said, drawing everyone's attention. "Will there be any more shopping stops?" He fussed with his pack and then slid it out of sight on the floor in front of him.

"Does that interest anyone else?" Robin asked, and a few people raised their hands. "Then what Johan can do after we get back from Burg Eltz is drive us back to the pedestrian zone of Trier for any last shopping. After that, it will be the day on the boat, then travel back to Frankfurt for the last-night celebration." He didn't want to disappoint anyone, but if they didn't have every souvenir possible by now, they were a little out of luck.

Johan pulled to a stop near the basilica, and Robin walked everyone over. Almost instantly they grew quiet as they entered the still-active church. He explained a little about the building and let people wander on their own. He always felt it important to let people discover things themselves.

"Be back in about twenty minutes," he added quietly, and waited while they looked around, then gathered everyone on the steps of the basilica. Johan joined them and took the pictures. A couple visiting the basilica was kind enough to take some pictures that included Johan. Then Robin led the group back to the bus.

They continued back to town and their hotel. Robin was never so happy to see the inside of a quiet room.

"I'm sorry you won't be with us on the boat trip," Robin said when Johan closed the hotel room door.

"It is the way it is. I will drive and meet you all in Koblenz." He seemed just as let down as Robin felt. "Have you given any thought to what will happen after this tour?"

Robin nodded. "I'm going to ask Albert if he will make you my permanent driver. And…." He bit his lower lip. "I want you to come home with me when I visit my mom and dad." That was a huge step. "I want them to meet you and get to know you." He could feel the shackles falling away from his heart and his resolve. "That is, if you want to."

Johan sat next to him. "How long will you stay there?"

"You won't come?" Robin asked when he heard Johan's phrasing of the question.

Johan nodded. "Yes, I will come, but I have to come back. I cannot stay. I can visit, but nothing more. I am not a citizen. You are and can come and go as you please."

"How about we go for a few weeks and then come back here? See how things work between us through

Christmas before making final decisions?" Robin was going to need to find some other kind of work. He could probably lead some holiday tours, but the tourist season would largely be done by Oktoberfest. "Maybe Albert can use me to help set up the tours for next year."

"So you'll stay?" Johan's grin split his face, his white teeth shining as they lit up the room.

"Yes. I have to get my medications filled when I get home and take copies of my prescriptions so I can get them refilled here. I'll also have to see my doctors and probably reassure my mother a million times, but I'm excited to have my own life." He had thought he'd be able to have one with Mason, and after that heartbreak, didn't think he'd ever be able to love again. Maybe that was the right decision and the one he'd made with Johan was stupid and ridiculous, but he wanted a life and a chance with Johan. If he were honest, what surprised Robin most was that Johan wanted to take a chance on *him*.

Johan engulfed him in a hug, holding him tightly. "I'm so happy." He kissed him, and Robin chuckled under his breath, returning his hug and pulling him down on the bed.

Robin blinked up at him, almost wondering how they'd gotten to this so quickly. Not that he was disappointed in any way.

"You have to know something. It's important that we all be happy, and I will take you lighting up my life for four days, four months, four years, or forty years." Johan swallowed hard, and Robin felt the beginning of tears prickling the edges of his eyes. "Whatever time we have together is precious."

Robin gulped, trying to pull oxygen into his lungs and failing for a few seconds. "You know that there is little possibility for forty years. We will never be able to grow old together."

Johan placed his hand flat on Robin's cheek, instantly heating the skin under it. "You and I don't know what the future will bring. But I do know I want you in mine." Johan slowly closed the distance between them. "So stop worrying about tomorrow. None of us knows what will happen."

"But I have to. I know I don't have that many tomorrows, and… if you set your heart on me, you will get hurt." Robin knew he'd explained this before, but Johan had to understand what he was getting into.

"You stress way too much," Johan told him with a wry curve to his lips. "Worry less, love more."

Robin had no argument to that, and Johan kissed away any potential protest as he slowly divested Robin of his clothes.

They came together with Robin on his back, watching as Johan's powerful chest heaved, small beads of sweat glistening on his golden skin as they made love. Johan's lips sent shivers of delight through him as they kissed and then as he found magical places Robin never knew existed until Johan touched them, adding to the exquisite pleasure of their joining. It was all Robin could do to hold on to Johan, using him as a rock, clinging to him to keep from flying into a million pieces, the excitement too great for one person to bear alone. Johan slowly, deliberately drove him to magnificent heights, the likes of which most people only dreamed were possible, and then light burst through him as their release broke like an epic, perfect wave bathing them in warmth.

Robin didn't dare move for a second. There was no way he wanted this spell to pop, but life outside the hotel room continued.

He jumped at the sharp knocks on the door, and Johan got off the bed with a sigh and tossed him a towel before grabbing his clothes and heading to the bathroom. He closed the door as Robin pulled on his pants and T-shirt, then went to answer the knocking.

"Billy," Robin said gently, but he wanted to scream and tell him to go away.

"Oh God," Billy said, his hand slapping over his mouth as his eyes flitted into the room. "I'm sorry, I didn't want to…." He seemed rooted on the spot, stammering. "I didn't know… I…."

Robin turned and got a clear view of the very messy bed, pillows askew, a sock hanging off the edge of the bedside table. He sighed. "It's all right. Give me a few minutes." Robin figured he probably had some kind of just-fucked glow, and really… it wasn't that he cared. He felt amazing and wasn't going to apologize for it. Still, he quickly cleaned up, then stepped out of the room and closed the door. Billy seemed more at ease and led the way down the hall. He opened the door to his room, and they joined Kyle inside.

"I saw him today," Billy said. "I saw Mason in a jewelry store. The one on the corner. He was looking at rings, and I heard him say he was getting married and needed an engagement ring. He said he wanted something more European. It was a load of—"

"I get the idea."

Kyle stood next to Billy, putting an arm around him. "It's okay. Take a deep breath and tell him what happened."

"Well, Mason was looking at this set of rings, and he asked to see some others. He was still looking at them, and the salesgirl brought out additional ones. He looked at those and told her he was going to have to think on it. She put them away and he left. After he left, I looked at the case, and three of the spots in one of the cases were empty."

"Did Mason know you were in the store?" Robin asked.

"I think so. I wasn't trying to hide, and he came in after me. I was looking at a watch." Billy's gaze shifted to the floor. "They were too expensive and I can't get one, but everything was so pretty that I wanted to look around."

"Do you think Mason took them?" Even as Robin asked, he was afraid he already knew the answer.

"I didn't see him do it, but then I suppose if I had, he wouldn't be a very good thief. Anyway, I suspect that they have cameras and things, so when they discover the things missing, they'll look and figure out that it's him."

"Yeah, and tomorrow we'll be out of town, and the day after that, on a boat and well away from here among a group of ever-changing tourists." Robin met Billy's and Kyle's gaze as he thought. "Tonight at dinner, you sit with Mason and keep him busy."

"Are you going to see what you can find in his room?" Kyle whispered, as though Mason could hear through the walls.

"Don't worry about what I'm doing. Just keep Mason there as long as you can. Buy him a drink if you have to, just try to get me some time." This whole situation was maddening, and he needed to do something about it. Robin didn't have any proof. He could call the police based on their suspicions, but then if they found nothing, he'd feel like a fool. No, he had to know what was going on and then he could take action from there.

"We'll do our best," Billy agreed, and thankfully didn't ask any more questions.

Robin left the room and returned to his own, where Johan waited for him, sitting on the edge of the bed, his leg bouncing nervously.

"What are you up to?" Johan asked as soon as Robin closed the door. "Something is not right." Johan patted the bed next to him, turning his attention to the wall to the adjoining room, which happened to be Mason's.

"Billy and Kyle are going to sit with Mason at dinner and keep him busy. I'm going to figure out a way to get into his room and see what he has in that pack of his. Billy might have seen him stealing again today, and we have to know. This entire thing is getting out of hand. If he is a thief, then we'll call the police, and they can take care of him." He was so tired of Mason causing trouble in his life, and now for the nice people on his tour.

"Okay," Johan agreed, and Robin did a double take. He'd expected Johan to fight him on it. "You will go down to dinner, and I will excuse myself after I make sure Mason sees me in the room. Then I'll return upstairs and check things out. You are too visible—everyone will wonder where you are. I'll come back down when I'm done." Johan took Robin's hand.

"Johan… I-I…." He stammered a little to get his thoughts together.

"How are you going to get into his room?" Johan asked, and Robin had to admit he hadn't really thought of that. "Don't worry. I'll be fine, and I know how to take care of things."

Robin narrowed his eyes. "How will you?" he questioned, and his only answer was a knowing grin that set Robin's belly fluttering. "Johan…."

"I promise I'll tell you all about my sordid past later tonight." He leaned closer, kissing Robin. "I hope that doesn't change your mind about me."

"What, that you have some mystery about you?" Robin snickered. "I think I like knowing there's something sordid about you. At least I know you aren't so damn perfect all the time."

Johan tugged him closer. "Come on. We need to get ready to go downstairs, and I have a little caper I need to get ready for." Johan pressed him back on the bed. "I need to be relaxed and stress-free."

"Oh, you do?" Robin teased. He could get used to the way Johan set about relieving stress. Especially as Johan's hands slid up under his shirt, fingers lightly plucking his nipples as he kissed him hard. This he could really get used to.

ROBIN WALKED into the simple but clean and rather bright hotel dining room. He purposely chose a seat where he could see Billy, Kyle, and Mason. They had given him some quizzical looks when he sat down, and Robin wondered how he would communicate to them the change in plan. Johan had joined him as well, but as soon as Mason took a seat with his back to Robin's table, Johan had quietly left the room. Robin hoped Billy saw him. If nothing else, Billy was talking a mile a minute, and whatever he was saying seemed to have captured Mason's attention, which was about the only thing that kept Robin from biting his fingernails down to the damn quick.

He did his best not to constantly look toward the doorway as a server took drink orders, while another set bowls of various salads at each table. The conversation level died down as people began eating.

Grant rushed in and sat across from him, startling Robin, who hadn't realized he was missing. Shit, he hoped Grant hadn't seen anything.

"Where's Johan?" Grant asked, and Robin hoped Mason didn't hear him.

"He remembered that he needed something at the *Apotheke*, so he rushed out to get there before they close." That seemed like a good excuse, but he knew he was probably pushing it at this hour. Hopefully anyone listening wouldn't know the difference. "Did you enjoy the day?"

"I did. It was great seeing all the Roman-era things. I had done some research so I knew what was in town, but it was stunning to see it all in person." Grant smiled and filled a plate from the bowls of carrot, potato, lettuce, and cabbage salad. Robin took a little himself, stifling the instinct to glance at the door. He had to remember not to draw attention to Johan's absence.

"I think you're going to love tomorrow, then. The history on display at Eltz is really stunning. Are you studying history?"

Grant nodded. "I'd like to become a professor and teach at a college." He took a bite of carrot salad and set his fork down. "But all I seem to do is memorize facts and spew them back on command. It's all my mind is good for. History is supposed to be more than that, though, and I seem to never know how to contextualize it."

Robin didn't know what to tell him, but he felt he needed to say something. "To me, history is about the people. Today we saw the Porta Nigra and learned that there was no mortar used in its construction. So the men who built it had to be very skilled and precise, using tools and skills from two thousand years ago. Every block cut by hand, every iron clip forged by a man with a fire and anvil." He smiled. Robin definitely had Grant's attention. "All of the buildings we've seen and marveled at were built by men like us. They lived their lives and did their best to support their families. The funny thing that a lot of people forget is that even the great artists, who loved what they did, were trying to make a living too, just like the rest of us."

"You know, that's a pretty cool way of looking at things."

"We like to think that everything happens for a reason, and most things do. But sometimes not for the reasons we like to think. There were originally four Roman gates to Trier. Only the Porta Nigra survives, because the interior was converted into a church. The others were carted away, stone by stone, to build other things over the centuries. So sometimes things come down to us through the centuries almost through no fault of their own. It doesn't mean the Porta Nigra was any better or more important than the others. Someone used it for a church, so it was preserved." Robin ate his salad and did his best not to fuss and worry.

When Mason stood and set his napkin on the table and turned to leave the room, Robin wondered how he could pull out his phone and message Johan without being obvious. He realized he couldn't and had to sit still, talking to Grant about God knew what because his head was somewhere else completely.

Billy turned and shrugged, looking worried as he too glanced at the door. There was nothing Robin could do except fret, and from experience he knew that was never good for him. Robin just had to eat and pretend that everything was okay.

"Sorry. The run took longer than I expected," Johan said, striding into the room and taking his seat at the table. He drank some water and filled a plate with salad before digging in. Apparently breaking into hotel rooms was hungry business. Of course, there was no way in hell Robin could ask him if his snooping had been a success, so he ate as well.

A thump from the floor above made Robin jump. Johan patted his leg under the table and continued eating as though he hadn't heard anything.

Mason returned a few minutes later, his face red, eyes darting around the room.

"What else have you found fascinating so far?" Robin asked Grant, pulling him into a conversation.

"Well, I guess I was surprised by how fast the Renaissance spread northward. Most of us don't think of people traveling that far in their lifetimes, but Dürer was a contemporary of Da Vinci, and they were both doing amazing things, so the ideas must have traveled pretty swiftly. I hadn't realized how quickly."

"Why is that?" Robin asked.

"Boats," Johan said. "People used boats. A lot faster than over land." He continued eating, and Grant nodded as though he had his answer. "Though the farther north you went, the longer the ideas took to spread."

He and Grant then went off on further discussion. It was interesting watching Grant's expression as it went from surprise to awe as they talked as equals. Johan was so much more than just a bus driver. Hell, if this were ancient Greece, Robin figured Johan could be Aristotle or Plato. At least he could be one of their contemporaries.

The servers brought plates of schnitzel and fried potatoes, setting them in front of everyone, as Robin studied Mason from the back. It was pretty clear to Robin that he was trying to appear relaxed, but his back was rigid, and the way he fidgeted in the chair indicated he desperately wanted to be somewhere else. Robin glanced at Johan, who shrugged and continued talking and eating.

"Maybe I can come back here when it's time for my dissertation. I would love to do some original research here."

"That would be very interesting. There are a number of libraries and repositories that you could get access to if you have academic credentials," Johan explained. "A lot of the professors here have colleagues in the US that they are close to. So you need to make connection there, and hopefully you can meet someone who can help open doors for you." Johan finished his salads and ate the rest of his dinner slowly.

Dessert was a small dish of ice cream. Robin picked at his, his leg bouncing under the table. Finally Johan was done eating and pushed back his chair. Robin did his best not to appear anxious and left with him. He expected Johan to head upstairs, but instead he left the hotel, and Robin followed him.

"I did not want the walls to have ears," he said. Sometimes his use of Americanisms was adorable. Johan reached into his pocket and pulled out a small box. "I believe these are what Mason stole today." He opened it. "We need to check with Billy, and then I thought we can look up the address and send them back. I did not actually touch them with my bare hands, but from what you told me, these have to be them."

"What are we going to do about Mason?" Robin asked as they continued walking.

"I don't know. That bag of his was full of small stuff—silver pieces, some gold, coins—whatever it seemed was small and he could lift. The man must be some kind of gifted, because there was a lot of it. His luggage had stuff in it too, but I heard someone on the stairs. These were right in the bag, so I grabbed them. I probably should have left them, but you said that Billy told you he thought Mason had taken the rings. At least the merchant here in Trier can get them back." Johan sighed. "They're a small business, and this kind of loss could set them back for months or mean their entire selling season is for nothing." Johan paused and turned to him. "We can probably come up with some way to send this back once Billy has had a chance to confirm if this is the stuff Mason took from the store."

"What if he doesn't know?" Robin asked.

"I don't know. I didn't think of that. All I did was think we could get this back to the store so they don't suffer." Johan swore softly in German. He put the box back into his pocket, and they walked back toward the hotel.

"I agree. We can come on Burg Eltz that way and take the road along the river for the best view," Robin said as they approached the front, in case anyone was listening.

They headed upstairs together, and Johan continued down the hall to Billy and Kyle's room and knocked on the door, while Robin entered the room he and Johan shared. He sat on the edge of the bed, listening for any sounds from Mason's room. He thought he heard him moving around, but he wasn't sure.

Johan returned and sat next to him, wrapping the box in paper and using his phone to get the address. Then he left the room without saying anything.

Robin listened once again and nearly jumped out of his skin when someone knocked sharply. "Yes," he said quietly through the door, fear rising in his throat. It would have been best if Johan hadn't touched anything and had just reported back what he'd seen. Now Robin was as jittery as he ever could remember being.

"Robin."

He swallowed hard at Mason's voice. "Give me a minute," he answered, moving through the room, trying to sound busy. He pulled off his shirt and cracked the door open, peering through, letting Mason see that he might be naked. "What's wrong, Mason?" he asked as innocently as he could. Maybe he and Johan should just call the police and let them deal with the whole mess. "I'm about to clean up and lie down."

"I wanted to ask you something. Can I come in?" Mason pressed.

"Now isn't a good time. Like I said, I'm going to clean up. Is there a problem with the hotel or the tour?"

"No… it's…." Mason glared at him, and Robin smiled as though he hadn't seen it at all.

"Can it wait until morning? We'll have plenty of time to talk on the bus or when we're out and about. I'm really tired, and I need some rest so I can make sure the group has a good time tomorrow." Hell, he wasn't above playing up his condition if it would get Mason to leave him alone.

"Mason," Johan said, and Robin angled so he could see him coming down the hall. "How can I help you?" Johan stood behind him, and Mason seemed to lose some of his assurance. "Robin is going to rest, but if you need something, I'll try to help you."

"No. I can talk to him in the morning." Mason brushed past Johan, who came into the room and locked the door.

"What did he want?" Johan asked, his eyes raking over him.

Robin felt his usual instinct to cover himself. It would take some getting used to before he felt comfortable being bare in front of Johan. Slowly he relaxed his arms. "He said he wanted to talk, but the desperation and panic in his eyes made me shiver. I was running out of excuses to keep him out."

Johan narrowed his eyebrows. "Why are you shirtless?"

"I tried to convince him that I was about to take a shower, but he was still being pushy." Robin moved into Johan's arms. "Until you came." He hugged Johan tightly. "This is really unnerving, and I'm sorry I got either of us involved." He closed his eyes, resting his head on Johan's chest before pushing away.

"What are you doing?"

"Cleaning up, in case he's listening." Robin stepped into the bathroom and closed the door. He undressed and readied himself to get into the tub.

The bathroom door opened and a naked Johan came in, stepped into the tub, and lowered the plunger. The tub filled, and Johan settled in the water, stretching out, and guided Robin between his legs.

"See, isn't this a lot better?" Johan purred into his ears, dripping water over his chest. "Just lean back and relax." Johan wrapped Robin in his arms, washing and holding him.

Robin quickly grew comfortable and relaxed, stretching out as much as he could, lightly running his fingers up and down Johan's legs. "I can't really remember the last time I took a bath. With the surgeries and scars, I had to be careful about getting them wet for a long time, so I took quick, careful showers instead." Robin chuckled softly. "Not that I ever had anyone to take baths with. Mason never took a shower or a bath with me. Not that I'd have been really keen on that prospect anyway."

"Hey. You're beautiful, and that's all that matters. The rest of it—Mason, your body issues—remember, I see you for you." Johan leaned forward to capture Robin's lips in a deep kiss. "It's just you and me, and Mason is part of the past. Let's keep him there."

Johan washed him slowly. There was an undertone of desire, but little overtly sexual about his touches. This was just being together, held, quiet—loved. Robin closed his eyes, reveling in the tenderness of the moment. He sighed softly, letting Johan take care of him until the water grew cold.

Robin climbed out and wrapped himself in a towel, leaving the bathroom. He pulled on some sleep clothes before lounging on the bed to watch television for a little while. Johan joined him a few minutes later, and they sat together, with Robin curled close to Johan, happy and content…

Until he realized they weren't alone.

CHAPTER 7

ROBIN STIFFENED from a doze, knowing something was wrong. Johan breathed deeply next to him and the room was quiet, but still, something wasn't right.

"Where is what you took from me?"

The light on the table clicked on, and Robin blinked at the sudden brightness as Mason stalked over to the bed. "What are you talking about?" Robin asked automatically, rubbing his eyes and forcing his brain into gear.

"You took something from my bag, and I want it back. Now." The panic rising in Mason's voice said plenty about his state of mind.

"And what would that be?" Johan asked with a seemingly clearer head than Robin's.

Robin pulled the bedding upward to cover himself and Johan, using it like a shield. "Mason, what's going on?"

"Don't play dumb with me. I know you left the dining room when I wasn't looking and then came back, and I know you were in my room. Do you think I wouldn't have a way of knowing?" Mason came closer, and Johan leaped out of the bed, his body taut and as ready to strike as Mason. As they squared off, Robin tried to figure out how he could get to his phone on the bedside table without Mason seeing him.

"We don't know what you're talking about. I had to go to the drugstore to get something before they closed, and if you have a guilty conscience, that isn't our problem. But it does beg the question of what you're so defensive about and what you've been up to."

"My business is my business." Mason glanced toward the door, probably trying to figure a way out of this. Johan stepped away, giving Mason the out, but he didn't take it. "And it would have been best if you two had stayed out of it."

"Mason, we don't know anything," Robin said, his legs quivering. "You need to leave now."

"I'm not going anywhere until I get what I came for," he hissed, pulling a knife. It wasn't big, but it gleamed in the reflected light and definitely gave Mason the advantage. At that moment Robin wished he'd taken Albert's advice and just called the police and been done with it. But Johan had recovered the rings, with the best of intentions, and they wanted to get them on their way back before calling the police. And now everything was a mess and both of them were in danger.... God, he'd been so stupid. If Mason could get into locked cases, he certainly could get into their hotel room. Robin most definitely didn't think like a criminal, that was for sure.

"But we don't know what you want," Johan pressed and stood still, in only a pair of light blue sleep shorts.

"Just go before you cause even more trouble," Robin added, motioning to the door. "This is ridiculous."

"No." Mason stepped forward, waving the knife. "I know you took them, and I want them back. Just give them to me and I'll be gone. Neither of you will see me again, and you can tell the tour whatever you like. Just hand them over." His eyes were wide, his pupils dilated.

"I can't give you what we don't have," Johan explained, trying to sound reasonable, his leg shaking a little. Robin was scared half to death for him. This situation wasn't going to be able to stay the way it was for very much longer.

A knock on the door made them all jump.

"Are you okay?" Billy asked through the door.

"No. Call the police, now!" Robin half yelled, and turned to Mason. "It's over. Whatever you've been doing is over. Put down the knife."

"No." Mason drew his hand back, and Robin braced for him to throw the knife. He had no idea if it was coming at him or Johan. Light gleamed off the blade as it sailed through the air, straight at him, but then *thunk*ed to the floor in a whirl of motion. Robin wasn't sure what had happened until blood bloomed and ran down Johan's arm. He'd batted the knife away to save him.

Johan clutched the cut on his arm, and Robin saw red, the entire room narrowing to Mason. Just reacting out of rage on Johan's behalf, Robin leaped, crashing into Mason, sending him thumping into the wall. "You shit! You hurt Johan!" Robin beat on Mason, kneeing and slugging with everything he had.

"Robin," Johan said from behind him. "I need your help."

That pulled him out of the dark place he'd slipped into. Robin looked down at Mason's bloodied face and his body curled into a fetal position. Robin hurried to the bathroom, grabbed a towel, and wrapped Johan's arm.

"Is it bad?"

"Not really," Johan said. "I don't think it's deep, but it's a long cut."

Robin got him sitting on the side of the bed and opened the door. The entire tour group had gathered outside.

"I called the police," Billy said.

"We need medical assistance too," Robin explained, and Billy got on the phone.

Mason groaned and tried to get up, but Kyle and Billy held him down until the police arrived, sirens splitting the night.

Robin explained what Mason had wanted, and officers went through Mason's room and removed all his things, carrying them out of the hotel in large, clear plastic bags. Lily fretted over both of them while Grant brought them each a bottle of water. Johan and Robin answered a million questions, neither of them saying a word about their little excursion earlier that night. It was probably best to leave that part out.

"Do you know what he was doing?" Robin asked the policeman wearing a sharp blue uniform. The man wasn't large but was still intimidating as all hell.

"It seems he was using the tour as a cover for his illicit activities," he explained in heavily accented English.

"We'd noticed that his pack was often full and then sometimes seemed empty," Robin explained nervously.

He'd been allowed to dress and stood in the hall while they helped Johan, who it seemed didn't need to go to a hospital. They were able to close the wound and had wrapped it for him, which was a huge relief. Robin gave the officer a copy of their itinerary so he'd know where they had been, and hopefully the recently stolen items could be returned.

The officer took notes and got their contact information. He checked Robin's identification, which he thought pretty standard. "You suspected him?"

"Yes. But we weren't sure," Robin answered. "Apparently something came up missing, and he thought we had taken it. We intended to call the police if we saw something definite, but we were never really sure what was going on. It would look bad for the tour company if I called the police on someone in my group and it turned out to be nothing." Robin wrinkled his brow. "Is there anything else we can do to help?"

"I do not think so," the officer said, and he left the room, Billy and Kyle going with him.

Once the medical personnel were done with Johan and packed up and left, Robin got him comfortable on the bed, which was blessedly free of blood. After Johan was settled, Robin went down to explain what had happened. The manager didn't seem happy, but there was nothing Robin could do. He thanked him for his help and wished him a good night, then stayed nearby until Billy and Kyle came back upstairs, meeting them in the hall.

"Please, everyone, go back to bed and get some rest."

"Will we be able to still go to the castle tomorrow?" Grant asked.

Robin wasn't sure if Johan would be able to drive, but he suspected he would if he was careful. "Right now our schedule hasn't changed. We'll meet in the morning. If we aren't able to use the bus, we can get to Moselkern by train and walk to the castle." It was a beautiful hour-long walk through the woods. Robin had done it before but hoped against hope that Johan would feel up to driving. "I have a backup if we need it."

He waited until all the others were in their rooms before going in to check on Johan. He found him in bed, lying on his back, bandaged arm outside the covers. "You scared the heck out of me."

"Me?" Johan asked, trying to sit up. "You went at him like a man possessed. I was afraid he'd hurt you."

Robin turned out the light and soothed him back down. Then he stripped off his clothes and got into bed, being careful not to jostle Johan. "Mason is a big, fat coward. He talks huge, but when it comes to anything physical, he backs off fast. I had to wait until he no longer had the knife and then I could go after him. You, on the other hand, scared the crap out of me."

"I had to stop the knife. I didn't mean to get cut myself." Johan closed his eyes, and Robin settled as best he could. "I'm going to be okay. It hurts, but it could have been worse for both of us." He sighed. "The police have Mason in custody, and he isn't going to be going anywhere very soon. He's a foreigner, so they aren't going to let him out on any sort of bond because he'll run. So jail and then court are waiting for him." Johan grinned. "Hopefully his victims will get their things back."

"Maybe. Who knows how much he's already sold?"

"True." Johan yawned. "Let's try to get some rest. We still have a big day ahead of us tomorrow, and I don't want to be driving anyone off the road." He gently turned on his side, and Robin pressed his leg next to Johan's, needing to touch him but not wanting to be close enough that he bumped his arm.

It took a while, but eventually he dozed off, though he woke again at every noise.

ROBIN GOT an awful night's sleep and left Johan in bed, dressing as quietly as he could before taking his pills and heading down to breakfast. The night's excitement was all the talk, and Robin gathered everyone together.

"Johan is still in bed, and I want to let him sleep for a while." He explained to everyone what had happened and what Mason had apparently been doing, intent on quashing any rumors. "Mason won't be with us going forward. What I'd like to do is give you all a few hours on your own this morning, and then once Johan has slept, we'll go to the castle. They have a wonderful café, and if you're all agreeable, we can have lunch there and then take our tour. Does that sound okay?" He waited, and everyone seemed fine with it. "Awesome." The group filtered off to do their own thing.

He got to work, making calls and canceling Mason's hotel room for the rest of the trip, which took a while. It would save Albert some money. Then Robin placed a call to Albert as well.

"Is Johan okay?" he asked as soon as Robin explained what had happened. "Can he drive?"

"He says so, and we're continuing on from here. Mason's rooms have been canceled going forward, so we're okay there." Robin went through his notes. "I think I can take care of everything else from here on. I just wanted you to know about our little excitement."

Robin figured he could fill Albert in completely once the tour was over.

"All right. You be careful, and don't let him overdo it. I expect the police will be in touch with us as well." Albert didn't seem upset at all, which was a little strange. He was concerned, though.

"I thought you'd be angry," Robin said.

"As long as everyone is okay, then we're good. And that takes care of the asshole ex-boyfriend."

Robin sighed. "Yes, it does."

"I have to take another call. There are actually people still booking for tours later this summer." He sounded so damned relieved. "But I have to be honest, I'm not sure if the company will be offering tours next year. Folks are going on their own… or with regular, nongay tours."

Robin wasn't sure what to say to that. He hadn't thought that far ahead, but it was probably time he found some other kind of work anyway. He needed to figure some shit out for himself. He really had no idea why this was so hard for him. He spent much of his free time thinking about what he was going to do and why he was holding back.

Robin hung up and sat in the lobby, ruminating on what had happened and what he had yet to do. He also worried a great deal about Johan but resisted the urge to go check on him. He wanted to give Johan as much a chance to rest as possible.

Johan came down a half hour before they were to leave, and after Robin made sure Johan was okay—more thoroughly than was probably necessary—Johan went right to the bus. Robin got on once Johan pulled it around. They waited for the others, and then they were off.

Johan was in pain; Robin saw it on his face, though he said nothing. Once they'd parked at the lot for the castle, Robin led the group down the path, leaving Johan to relax. As soon as they rounded the corner and viewed the castle perched below them on the bluff, a quiet came over the entire group. It was awe-inspiring, not because of its size, but its sheer ancient rustic beauty. This was living history right before them.

"Once you've taken your pictures, I'll lead you down and set you up with tickets. You tour on a time basis, and we will probably have to wait about an hour."

"So we'll have time for lunch?" Javier asked.

"Yes. Now, when it's time to come back, we'll gather and wait for the shuttle to take us to the parking lot. We'll be going downhill to get there, so it's all uphill returning."

They walked down and through the castle gate. Robin got tickets for the group and showed them to the café, where everyone gathered in small groups at the tables. Robin sat alone, looking at his phone, surprised he had service at all. After checking the time, he messaged his mother and received an immediate response, so he called.

"Hey, Mom," he said quietly, and pressed the button for FaceTime after she told him she had gotten a new iPhone. It was great being able to share this with her. "Look where I am." He turned away and panned the phone. "You remember?"

"Yes." She smiled as he returned her to voice only, not sure how long the other connection would last. "Are you okay? You look tired."

"I am. It was a rough night." He didn't go into details. His mother would freak, and that wasn't going to do either of them any good. "Anyway, I wanted to tell you that when the tour season is over, I asked Johan to come back with me so he can meet you."

"You did?" she asked with surprise.

"I like him, Mom, but I'm scared… I guess. I want him to come meet you, and I'm scared he's going to wake up any day and realize that I'm as dull as dirt and not worth all the heartache that is going to come eventually." He rambled a little and hoped his mom understood half of what he was saying.

"Slow down. First, I'm happy, and your father and I would love to meet anyone important in your life. You know that." She paused, and Robin waited as she gathered her thoughts together. "As for all this heartache stuff… I assume that's because of the transplant."

"Yeah…."

"Okay. Let me ask you something. If Johan told you he had a disease that meant he was only going to live for a year or two… would you walk away?"

"No. I love him, Mom, and I'd—"

"Then why would he?" his mother interrupted, and Robin stopped short. "You definitely need to bring this man home so we can meet him and stop all this worrying. As a kid, you spent more time worrying about what everyone else thought, and we all had to try to figure out what you wanted. Just go after what you want and let the rest go. Johan gets to make his own decisions, just like you do."

"So you're happy for me?" Robin asked as he tried to swallow around the lump in his throat.

"Of course I am. You deserve love, the same as anyone else, and if this Johan is it, then both your father and I will be happy to welcome him into the family."

Billy came over, standing near the table.

"I have to go, but I'll call you soon. And thanks. That was just what I needed to hear."

"Love you, sweetheart," his mother said, and then they ended the call.

Billy asked him a quick question about when they were supposed to be back, then rejoined Kyle.

Robin sat at the table in the sunshine, the breeze whispering around him, and instantly he wanted to be back on the bus with Johan. He understood now. In many ways Johan was the person he'd always dreamed of: strong, intelligent, brave, patient…. Why wouldn't he be willing to accept what Robin was able to give?

Robin bit his lower lip, looking at the rest of the group. They were all talking happily, excitement running through them, something he remembered from the first time he came here.

"You look ready to fly apart," Oliver said as he placed his tray on the table and sat. Javier sat across from him. "I hope this is okay. It's the only table left."

"Of course." Robin pulled his thoughts out of where he wanted to be and returned to where he was. "Just woolgathering."

Javier snickered. "I think the entire group knows where your thoughts are right now." He leaned closer to Oliver. "And none of us would blame you for a second." He shuffled his chair so he was closer to Oliver. "Being with someone you think the world of is worth it, no matter what." He sighed softly. "I know Oliver is older, but I intend to see to it that he lives a good long time, because I'll be damned if I'm going to let him go."

Robin screwed up his courage. "Do you mind if I ask you something? What if he told you that he had a disease that will only allow him to live, say, four or six more years? What would you do?"

Javier swallowed his bite of sausage and looked Robin square in the eye. "The first thing I'd do is hold him tight, and the second would be to ask him to make a list of everything he wanted to see and do. Then we'd start doing all of them together." Javier took Oliver's hand. "I wouldn't waste a moment. I almost made the biggest mistake of my life when things got difficult between us. I won't let that happen again, and if what you said were to happen, he and I would make as many memories as possible and enjoy whatever time we have left." Javier set down his plastic fork. "I take it that one of you—"

Robin nodded. "There is only so much time."

"Then why are you wasting it sitting here wishing you were with him? Go on back to the bus. Oliver and I know what we have to do, and we'll get everyone back up there." He pointed toward the road. "The shuttle stops there, and our tour is in half an hour right through there."

"Be sure to go through the treasury as well. It's stunning and contains some of the most beautiful pieces from the castle." Robin was glad Mason wasn't with them. He could only imagine how worried he'd be with him in there.

"We aren't going to miss anything. Now go. It's fine."

Oliver and Javier shooed him away, and Robin walked across the bridge to the shuttle stop and took it back to the parking area. Johan sat on the bus, his head back and eyes closed. He hated to disturb him but knocked softly on the door. Johan opened it, and Robin got on board.

"What are you doing here? Are they done?" Johan sat up and looked ready for business.

Robin leaned down, kissing him hard. Johan stiffened, and Robin pressed more firmly, his tongue searching for entrance as he cupped Johan's rough cheeks.

"I take it not." Johan chuckled as Robin backed away a little.

"No. They have their tour in twenty minutes. I wanted to be up here with you. Oliver and Javier will make sure everyone makes it back to the bus." He was tempted to sit in Johan's lap, but he didn't want to hurt him.

"So you came back here to keep me company?" Johan's smile told Robin he was pleased.

"Yes, and to tell you that I love you." Robin sat in the seat behind Johan, who joined him, sitting thigh to thigh. "I'm sorry I've been so thickheaded." He gently rubbed Johan's uninjured arm. "I talked to my mom, and she told me that she's looking forward to meeting you. She said that I needed to be happy." He met Johan's gaze. "I always thought she'd be angry if I didn't stay at home, but she surprised me."

"Is she why you're here now?"

Robin shook his head. "I'm here because I want to be happy. I'm not scared anymore. At least I'm not scared for me. And I guess I can let you be scared for you." He held Johan's arm, resting his head on his shoulder. "You're a hero. You rescued me from Mason, and you rescued my heart from cold disuse." Robin sniffed and wiped his eyes with his free hand.

Johan turned to him, confused. "Why do you think that?"

"I was given a new heart…. In a way, I get to borrow the rest of someone else's time, and I figure I should make the most of it. I was worried that I would hurt whoever I loved. I was always concentrating on the negative." He sighed. "That's so fucking easy to do."

Johan scoffed. "For you, maybe." He was teasing, and it was nice… in a way.

"For most of us who aren't perfect knights in shining armor, being positive is hard."

Johan put an arm around his shoulder, and Robin nestled close for a while. "I know you've been through a lot of pretty unfair things. But…."

"I know. You decided you'd be happy and that was that." Robin knew it probably wasn't that simple.

"No. I almost died too once."

Robin pulled away, glaring at him. "Why didn't you tell me before?"

Johan rolled his eyes. "I wanted you to like me for me… not because we had some supposedly life-changing experience in common. See, I liked you before I knew what you'd been through, and I wanted you to like me the same way." He shrugged and rolled his eyes as though that was so obvious.

"Man, I think you're going to surprise me when I'm eighty," Robin quipped, and Johan stared at him, his eyes wide and his mouth hanging open. "What?"

"That's the first time you have ever mentioned growing old. You always say that will never happen." Johan touched the underside of his chin. "You always take care of yourself and you are active. You eat right, and maybe you are the person who lives for decades."

"Johan… I…."

"No. It has to be someone, so why not you? We will live whatever time we have together as though it is our last. That way we regret nothing." He drew Robin closer.

"Are you going to tell me what happened to you?" Robin asked.

"Does it matter?" Johan asked.

Robin thought about it, realizing it didn't at all. He shook his head, and Johan sat still and quiet, holding him as they waited together in the wooded parking lot. Robin had seen castles and mountains, the grandest cathedrals, and the world's most fabulous works of art, but nothing compared to the simple wooded view out of the front window of the bus… with Johan.

"I got meningitis when I was twelve. They didn't think I would live. I remember being only partly aware of what was happening around me. People coming and going, shots, tests—I suppose you know the whole drill."

Robin definitely did.

"I remember my mama crying at the side of my bed, and I tried to move my hand to pat her head. I wanted to tell her that it was all right, that I was going to be okay, but I couldn't. Then I must have slept or something. When I woke up again, it was quiet and Mama was there with me. She smiled when she saw me, and I told her '*trinken.*' I don't think I have ever seen my mama smile so big before. After that, I got better, but it took time. They told me when I was older that I almost died." Johan turned to look at him. "I never thought I would die, even when I was so sick. It was when I was older that it hit me, and I figured I'd been given a second chance." He rested their heads together. "I do understand second chances and being given something back."

Robin nodded and sat still. "I do love you."

"Me too, Liebling. That's the hard part. Now we only have to figure out what we're going to do about it."

Robin shrugged. "I have a tiny apartment in Frankfurt for the season. It isn't very big and is sort of quirky, but it's enough for the two of us."

Johan nodded. "Do you have to live there? We could live in Baden-Baden near my family. They could get to know you better, and I have an apartment… well, rooms above the restaurant there. Most of the family cooking is done there, so I only have a tiny kitchen, but there's a great view of the town from the upper floor, and it's mine. We could take the train when we need to go on a tour. It's much quieter and prettier than Frankfurt."

Robin didn't really mind where he lived. "I have to give them a month's notice, but…." He shrugged. "They can probably rent it quickly." Apartments were in high demand in most of Germany, so there was little chance of Robin being out too much.

"No doubt. You will like Würzburg, and my mother already likes you."

"I'll be gone quite a bit leading tours anyway, and after that, we can visit my family and figure things out from there." Maybe he and Johan would make Würzburg their permanent home. That wasn't the worst thing.

They sat quietly once again, Robin thinking of the things he had to pack as the group approached the bus. He had completely lost track of time. Johan returned to his seat, and Robin met the happy group as they got back on the bus.

"Did you have a great time?"

CHAPTER 8

THE TRIP up the Rhine should have been the most relaxing day of the tour. Once Robin got the group on the riverboat, they got to sit back and watch German history pass by. Castles, ruins, vineyards, and the Loreley all passed as they sat, ate, and drank a little, with something new to see around each and every bend. It should have been easy and restful, but Robin wished Johan was with him. It made the day a little less sunny, but they each had their jobs to do, and Robin told himself he needed to man up and quit whining to himself.

"How many times have you done this tour before?" Margaret asked as she and Lily sat next to him near the bow of the boat for the very best view.

"I think this is my sixth or seventh time, but it's some of the most amazing scenery in Europe." Robin pointed ahead as a small water castle came into view, built on an island in the river. "I always wanted that one right there. Boats going by all day, my own castle on an island." He smiled as they glided by, an automated tour recording explaining what they were seeing in German and then English.

"That would be awesome." Margaret turned to Lily. "This has been a great trip, but I think I'm getting to the point where I'm ready to go home."

Lily sighed. "You don't have to go back to the messy pieces of a divorce."

"Maybe not," Robin told her. "But, you aren't the same person you were that first day either."

"Yeah, you've seen castles and cathedrals, and went to a spa naked. You can kick the cheating bastard's ass." Margaret held up her glass, and Lily clinked it, smiling again.

"Sometimes I wonder if anyone is ever the same after seeing all this." Robin sat back in his chair. He wanted to close his eyes and doze, but that wasn't a good idea. "Think about it. Back home, the country is over two hundred years old, but some of these castles have been ruins for longer than that. Julius Caesar crossed this very river in an effort to conquer Germania. This land remembers the good and the bad. It's happened here, and people survived and flourished over centuries." He was feeling a little romantic and decided he'd probably said enough already.

"Does it change much from year to year?" Lily asked.

Robin shook his head. "Nope. This view is pretty much the same as when I first took this tour my first summer of college. It's one of the things I like most about it."

He scooted over as Grant, Oliver, and Javier joined them. Pretty soon most of the group had gathered together, watching the scenery slide past.

The day waned slowly and the sun eventually set behind the hills on the riverbank. Once they arrived at their final stop, they all got off, and Johan was there to meet them. As night fell, clouds rolled in, and once everyone was on the bus, huge drops pelted the windshield and sides.

"Was that a good time?"

"Awesome" seemed to be the word used most.

"We're going to head to dinner and then the hotel in Mainz. Tomorrow we'll look around the town before heading to Frankfurt, where we've arranged a special farewell evening. The drive isn't too long, so sit back and relax. Johan is going to turn out the lights so he can see better, and we'll arrive soon." Robin sat down and patiently waited as Johan navigated through the town and pulled up to the restaurant.

It was raining more heavily, and everyone hurried off the bus and inside to the dining room.

"Please sit down and relax. We're a little early, but they're doing what they can to accommodate us." Robin worked with the restaurant, and they began bringing out the food that was ready. Conversations started at the same time all over the room. Robin heard snippets about the cruise and all the things they'd done together.

"You did this," Johan said. "Look at them. They didn't know one another a week ago and now they're all talking like old friends. They've had fun, and maybe some of them have grown a little. Mostly they're a group now."

"Yeah, and tomorrow is the last day and then they go home."

"True. But some of them will stay in touch, and they'll all have great memories. That's what you gave them. A chance for something they'll be able to talk about for the next twenty years." Johan took his hand. "I know I'll remember this trip for a very long time." He grew quiet as their food arrived, and Robin and Johan ate schnitzel. It was a good thing he liked the stuff, because they tended to get it a lot.

"To schnitzel," Javier said, raising his glass.

The others all chuckled and toasted. There was strudel for dessert. It wasn't original, but it was good, filling, and Robin was glad for every single bite.

Unfortunately, the weather was such that going out was out of the question, but there were amusements in the lobby area, and everyone broke into groups, playing games, even doing a puzzle, and having a quiet night in.

"Come join us!" Lily called, and Robin pulled out a chair at the table. "It's Cards Against Humanity. I think it's the British edition, and it's hilarious. I have no idea who half these people are, and it's still funny."

Pretty soon everyone was gathered around the table having the time of their lives. Lightning flashed outside and thunder rumbled, but the laughter kept on well into the evening. It was a pretty amazing highlight of the day. Well, at least until Johan got him alone in their room. Apparently he was feeling better, and he carefully showed Robin just how special he was.

Thankfully the thunder drowned out most of the cries of passion.

THE LAST part of the tour went off swimmingly, and late the following afternoon, Johan pulled the bus up in front of the group's final hotel in Frankfurt. It was modern, relatively new, and probably the most uninteresting one they'd stayed at.

"How will we get to the airport in the morning?" Grant and Billy asked before getting off the bus.

Robin stopped everyone and made a general announcement. "The hotel has a service they contract with. I believe it's five euros a person, and all you need to do is talk with the desk clerk and they will arrange for the ride and contact you in the morning when they are ready to go. It's very easy and a bargain. Subway tickets will cost you almost as much. And you all know about the farewell dinner. The hotel has a dining room on the top floor, and we will meet there at seven this evening. That's nineteen hundred *Uhr* for all you who have gotten used to German time." He smiled and was met with happiness in return. "Johan and I will see you then."

Robin got off the bus, and the others followed. He made sure everyone got their luggage, Javier pitching in to help so Johan didn't hurt his arm.

"Where are you staying tonight?" Johan asked once everyone was inside and only the two of them stood next to the bus.

"At my apartment. I never stay at the hotel here in Frankfurt, to save Albert the expense." Robin smiled. "In a way I'm ready to be settled for a while. We pick up our next group in a few days and start this all over again."

"We don't start everything again…." Johan winked, and Robin smiled back. They already had a good start.

"No, we don't." Robin shifted closer, and Johan slipped his good arm around his waist. "But what are we going to do until dinner?"

"We could make out in the back of the bus?" Johan offered.

Robin snickered. As *interesting* as that sounded…. "Or we could wait and make love in my bed once we get back to the apartment." He leaned against Johan, sighing softly. "We still have a few hours, and I need to make phone calls."

"I need to get the bus back." Johan smirked. "Duty calls." He moved away and got back in the bus, then pulled out into traffic.

ROBIN ENDED up taking the subway to his apartment. He made his phone calls and opened the place up, letting it air out. He also turned on the refrigerator and made a quick run to the local grocery to get some food in the place. It was nice to be back.

Schnitzel the cat seemed pleased too, when he bounded in through the window, purring softly as Robin petted him.

"Yeah, I missed you too. But I bet Mrs. K is wondering where you are."

Schnitzel didn't seem to care, and after making himself comfortable in Robin's chair, he proceeded to fall asleep in the sun.

Robin changed and brought the cat to his grateful owner before taking the train back to the hotel and heading up to the top floor.

Everyone had gathered and the party had already started. A buffet dinner had been set up, and plates were being filled, the entire room alive with conversation.

Javier pressed a Schorle into Robin's hand. "This was a great trip. Just what Oliver and I needed." He held Oliver's hand and a wide grin split his face.

"You two have a safe trip home and be good to each other."

Their attention shifted to the door, and Robin turned as Johan came in, a vision in black pants and shirt.

"You do the same," Oliver said.

But Robin barely heard him. Johan strolled over and cupped Robin's cheeks. He kissed him right there, to whoops from the rest of the group and even a cry of "get a room," which set everyone laughing, considering they had been sharing one the entire trip.

Robin blinked when Johan pulled back and turned to the others, his cheeks heating.

"It's true…." Lily quipped. "The good ones really are gay."

"You better believe it, honey," Billy quipped back as he and Kyle shared a kiss that threatened to light a fire.

Robin slipped an arm around Johan's waist and leaned against him.

"To an amazing trip," Grant said, raising his glass. The others followed, toasting and drinking, and then the conversation began once again.

After everyone had a chance to eat, Robin stood and clinked his glass to get everyone's attention. "I want to thank you all for a memorable tour." He glanced at Johan, whose dark eyes grew steamy for a second. "I don't think I will ever forget it." He extended his hand, and Johan took it, standing beside him. "You were an amazing group, and it was a fun tour. I'm so glad you all seemed to enjoy it. I've sent a sheet around the room. Anyone who wishes can add their name and email address. I will then send a group email to those who sign up. That way you'll have addresses if you wish to contact each other."

"Have you heard anything about Mason?"

Johan cleared his throat. "I checked with the police in Trier, and they confirmed that they arc holding him on theft charges and working to get the items he stole back to their rightful owners."

Robin cleared his throat to try to change the subject. It was a party after all. "Please have a wonderful evening, and thank you all for coming along with me. I wish you all a safe and easy journey home." Robin raised his glass, and everyone did the same.

The conversation began again in earnest, and Johan turned to him, heat once again rising in his eyes. "How long do you have to stay?" He tugged Robin closer. "I don't want you to get too tired. I think we should go back to your apartment and not come out for days. I hope."

"Smooching on the job," Albert said as he came in, and Robin rolled his eyes as he backed out of Johan's embrace.

"Like you didn't have anything to do with this." He mock-glared at his boss before breaking into a smile.

Someone started glasses clinking, and the conversation died. Kyle cleared his throat. "Billy and I want to thank Johan and especially Robin for a great trip. Robin listens a lot and gives good advice."

"Kyle…," Billy said softly as Kyle took his hand, and Robin eased closer to Johan, putting his arm around his waist as excitement built.

"I know what and who I want in my life now. My eyes are open and I see you for all you are to me." Kyle pulled a small box out of his pocket. "I got this in Trier. It's a Roman coin." He slipped the chain over Billy's neck. "That coin is two thousand years old, and that's how long I promise to love you. Will you be my love and my life… forever?"

Billy's answer was lost as he launched himself at Kyle, and they embraced and kissed deeply.

Robin turned away and found Johan looking back at him. Love was definitely in the air. Oliver and Javier had moved closer together, Javier with his arm around Oliver's waist. The other couples had done the same, all standing together, happy, watching the newest pair join their loving ranks.

"Hey," Johan said softly, tilting Robin's head upward. "I see what you want."

Robin smiled. "I already have what I truly want." He swallowed hard. "And I want to grow old with him." Johan closed the distance between them.

EPILOGUE

The Following Spring

"LIEBLING," JOHAN soothed as Robin fussed through the apartment. He fluffed the pillows on the sofa and went into the second small bedroom to make sure the bed was perfect. "It's okay. Your mom and dad are going to have a good time, and they're going to be happy just to see you."

"I know, but it's been since last fall, and I'm looking forward to their visit. They haven't been back to Germany in a long time, and I want things to be perfect." Robin closed the bedroom door and checked through their small living room and kitchen.

"My parents are looking forward to meeting them, and I know your mom and my mom, they are going to spend hours together in the kitchen." Apparently the two of them had already been swapping recipes. "So don't worry. You spent all that time as tour guide, so you know where to take them without wearing them out. They're here for two whole weeks, so…."

Robin sat down and took a deep breath, checking his watch for the eighth time in almost as many minutes. "It's going to take us some time to get to the airport, and their flight lands in a few hours. I checked and it's running on time."

Johan took his hand. "Come on. If we get there early, we can stop for a Schorle."

Schnitzel jumped up on the sofa and crawled into Robin's lap, purring loudly as he made a nest for himself. "You ready to meet your grandma?"

Mrs. K had developed health issues a week before Robin was scheduled to move out, and she couldn't take care of Schnitzel any longer. Robin had agreed to take him. Johan still wasn't so sure, even though the cat adored him and followed Johan everywhere—or tried to. Sometimes Robin wondered if Johan rubbed fish on his clothes.

"We have to go, so you be good while we're gone." Robin lifted Schnitzel onto the cushions and stood to follow Johan out and down to the car. In the States, the Smart car would have been dwarfed by everything on the road, but here it was eminently practical, especially with the high cost of fuel.

They were met by Johan's parents. His dad tossed Johan the keys to his Mercedes and told him to take their car instead, since it would be more comfortable. "We will meet them here."

"I have special lunch planned," Johan's mom explained.

Robin hugged her. Greta had become a second mother to him. He loved her almost as much as his own. He and Fritz shared a love of fishing, and Fritz even showed Robin some of his favorites brooks for trout.

"Louisa is coming too." Marta was away at Princeton but would be home in a few months.

"Thank you." He loved how they had made him feel welcome, and they seemed to be extending those same feelings to his parents. "We have to go."

Robin got into the passenger seat of the plush, comfortable car, and Johan drove them to the Autobahn, opening the car up. They sailed at speeds unheard of in the US to the outskirts of Frankfurt, where they encountered traffic at the turnoff for the airport. Robin grew more nervous as they got out of the car and walked into the terminal, where they would meet Robin's parents once they landed and went through passport control and customs. According to the information board, the plane had landed twenty minutes earlier, so they would be coming out at any time.

"There they are," Johan said five minutes later, and Robin hurried over to hug his mom and then his dad.

"You're here!"

"You look wonderful," his mother said, holding his hands and taking a step back. "Whatever you're doing here agrees with you."

"I work from home most days, and Johan and I meet for lunch. He's helping his family with the restaurant, and I'm working with Albert to set up the tours for this summer. All of them are full, and we are adding one or two more to handle the demand."

Oliver, it seemed, had a huge circle of friends, and they had gotten the word out. Bookings had been coming in for months.

"I love it here, Mom."

“Son,” his dad said, and Robin hugged him again. “It’s so good to see you.”

“I’m glad you could get away.” This was the first vacation his parents had taken in years.

“Your brother has been taking over more and more, so we decided that he can handle things for a couple of weeks.” Dad leaned closer. “I think he’s happy to have us out of the way for a while.”

“Come on. Let’s get you to the car. We need to get back. Greta has lunch planned for you, and then you can rest after the long flight.” He took his mother’s bag, and Johan took his dad’s, and they walked out to the car. On the drive back, they talked a little but mostly let his parents rest in back.

After Johan pulled to a stop outside what was now Robin’s home, they helped get his parents’ things to their room.

“Mom said lunch will be ready in half an hour.”

Robin and Johan left his parents in their room and went to the living room. They sat on the sofa together, and Schnitzel took possession of Johan’s lap.

“Do you miss home?” Johan asked quietly.

Robin thought for a second and shook his head. “This is home. Mom and Dad live in the States, but Würzburg is home. You are home, and I don’t regret a thing. Yes, I wish I could see my mom and dad more often, but in the end, you are everything this borrowed heart of mine could ever want.”

Johan touched his chin, meeting Robin’s gaze. “The time you got from the transplant may have been borrowed, but the heart, your heart, that’s all you.”

KEEP READING FOR AN EXCERPT FROM

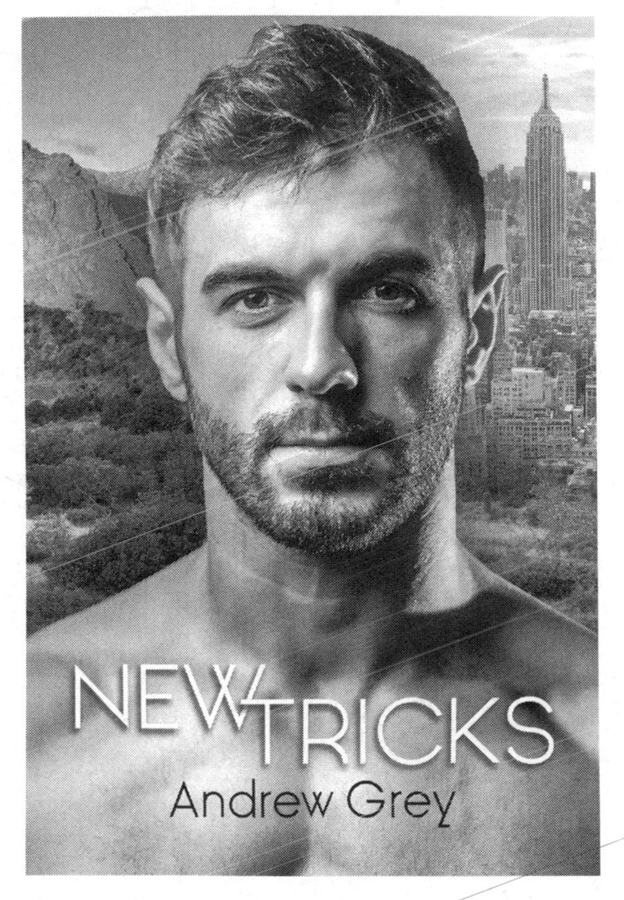

NEW TRICKS

By Andrew Grey

In matters of the heart, there's no such thing as business as usual.

Thomas Stepford spent years building a very successful business, and now at thirty-nine, he wants a quieter life. With his parents needing help, he decides to return home. He can't get away from business completely and needs an assistant—but the man who is hired isn't quite what he had in mind.

Brandon Wilson, the ink on his degree barely dry, needs a job, and his mother helps him get one as Mr. Stepford's assistant. Thomas doesn't seem to remember, but Brandon worked mowing the stunningly attractive older man's lawn years ago. Thomas was Brandon's teenage fantasy, and now he's Brandon's boss.

Thomas and Brandon are both determined to keep their relationship strictly business, but the old attraction is still there. They learn to work together even as the tension between them reaches the boiling point. But just as they start to surrender, Thomas's old life in New York calls him. Even if he resists that pull, can their newfound relationship survive when Brandon receives the call of his dreams... from Hollywood?

CHAPTER 1

"YOU'RE REALLY leaving," Blaze said as he sat down in front of Thomas's desk with a sigh. "Why in the hell would you want to do that? This is the land of guys, fun, and a million things to do, all of which will either get you laid or are on the path to getting you laid, and you're going to run back to… where is it exactly you're going?" He leaned forward a little just so Thomas could get a good look at the disbelief in his eyes. "Butt-fuck Egypt?"

Thomas shook his head slowly. "Colorado Springs, and I'm going back home to spend some time with my parents." He growled a little. "Don't you work for me? And since I know you do, why doesn't that insulate me from your whining and bitchiness?" Thomas groused, trying his best to seem upset. He knew it hadn't worked when Blaze simply rolled his eyes.

"Because I'm your best friend, have been since we were in Alpha Chi together, and yeah, you own the company, but you know it wouldn't be anywhere without my sparking personality to help smooth the way for all those deals you've made over the years." Blaze smirked, and Thomas glared at him. "You remember in college we both vowed we were going to make a huge splash in the world, a shitpile of money, and then we were never going to go back to those awful towns where we grew up?" He gave an exaggerated shiver.

Thomas shook his head. "I'm getting tired, Blaze. I built this firm to the point where it has more employees than the high school I attended, and all of them are very smart and know their jobs. Otherwise you and I would never have hired them. I'm only moving back to Colorado Springs, not to the moon, and I'm still going to run the company. I'm just going to do it from a place that's quieter and less… easy."

"Easy! You think New York is easy?" Blaze's eyes widened.

"Yeah, it is. Everything is here for the taking," Thomas countered. "It's too damned easy. There are guys—and girls, if that's your thing—around every single corner. If one won't suffice, just choose another one, or two, maybe three. If you have money, everything seems like it's for sale. And I'm tired of it. Okay? I want something slower." He swallowed and half closed his eyes. "I swear I haven't slept more than a few hours a day in the last eighteen years."

"So you're giving it up," Blaze pressed. "Just like that?"

"My parents are getting older. They haven't said anything, but I know they're going to need help soon. I want to spend some time with them and maybe build a life."

Blaze nodded. "I know what this is. You're still hurting from when Angus left, and you want to give yourself a change of pace. You know, the best way to get over a man is to find another one, and there are plenty of hot guys in New York who would fall all over themselves for the chance to try to win your heart."

Thomas frowned. Blaze didn't get it. "That's the problem. They're all interested, but I'm not. And for the record, I left Angus. There was nothing between us, and all he did was complain that I worked too much. Everyone I've ever dated has said the same thing: I spent too much time working and not enough time with them."

The desk phone buzzed, and Blaze stood. "That would be Marjorie, and I'm out of here before she sees me sitting with you and decides it would be a good time to tell me all the things I'm doing wrong in my life. Why can't that woman spend her time talking you out of this harebrained idea rather than torturing me?" Blaze tried to look innocent, but Thomas knew he and Marjorie got a perverse thrill out of annoying each other as much as possible.

Thomas waved Blaze off and answered the call.

"Your two o'clock meeting is waiting outside, and your two thirty called and is running a few minutes late. That means your three o'clock is going to be tight and—"

"We'll make it work. We always do." Thomas checked the clock as Blaze hightailed it out of the office. The only good thing about this appointment was that it got him out of talking more with Blaze about him moving closer to his family. Thomas knew that was going to be a sore subject for Blaze, whose parents had never accepted him for who he was. They still harbored delusions that he'd get over this gay phase of his life, settle down, and produce grandchildren for them. At least Thomas's parents were supportive… even if they drove him a little around the bend.

Thomas stood as his appointment came in, and he motioned toward the conference table. He listened to the proposal, which he really had no interest in, and by the end, he still saw no viable financial benefit for anyone.

He hoped the rest of the afternoon was going to be more productive.

Thankfully it was, and he got plenty done before emerging from his office after seven. Marjorie still sat at her desk, like a gatekeeper. "You don't need to stay this late. Go home and have some fun."

She scoffed, looking at him askance. "This coming from the man who gets here before everyone else and leaves later than most everyone. What are you going to do when you move and you don't have an office to sit in until well into the evening?" She smiled to show him she was only partially kidding.

"I don't know. Are you sure you won't come with me?" He'd already asked her four times, but was willing to try again.

"Yes. I'm sure. I'll hold things down for you here, and once you get to Colorado Springs, I'll help you find an assistant who can work with you there."

Meaning someone who wasn't going to drive Marjorie crazy. She liked things a certain way, and he loved that she was the most organized and efficient person he'd ever met. Marjorie always thought steps ahead so she could smooth the way and help keep him as efficient as possible. Thomas was going to miss her.

"Everything will be fine, and I'll even stop picking on Blaze… a little."

God, Thomas loved that twinkle in her eyes.

"And once you're gone, I promise to leave the office at five every once in a while."

Thomas chuckled. "Thank you." Leaving her was the one thing that worried him. He depended on her to keep his life organized and together so he could concentrate on the really important things. "Good night. I'll see you in the morning."

"Tomorrow is Saturday, and the movers are coming to start packing your things. I'll send a message to your phone so you don't forget." She smiled and waved as Thomas left the office.

He made it to the elevator before yawning, and leaned against the side of the elevator car for the ride down to the underground parking garage. He told his driver to stop at the bodega on the way home so he could get something to eat. He grabbed something to go and got back into the car for the ride to his apartment.

Thomas went inside and ate his dinner in front of the television, with some papers for company. For years he'd spent his time and energy building Stepford Management into one of the top real estate management and consulting firms in the country. Deal after deal, development after development—he and his teams put them together, brought them to fruition, and made a lot of money doing it. Thomas had more than he could spend now, and he was tired.

He used to look forward to going into the office. When he was younger, deals got him excited and kept him up at night. He used to dream of building towers and filling them with tenants, changing the face of the New York skyline. And he'd done all that. Thomas had worked with some of the biggest and most important people in the city of New York over the years, and he'd loved it. But now the thrill wasn't there anymore. It was just work, and he was self-aware enough to know he needed a change of pace. Something different, slower. He needed a chance to do something other than work.

His phone buzzed in his pocket, and he hauled it out. There was a message from his mother telling him that she seen to it that everything met his requirements and that everything was okay and looked good.

Thanks, Mom, he replied. His mother had taken to texting like a duck to water. She'd always hated talking on the phone, and now she sent messages all the time.

When are you leaving New York?

They're packing things tomorrow. I will fly out Tuesday once I have a few things settled in the office.

Good. The screen indicated that she was still composing a message, so he waited. *Is Marjorie going to come with you?*

No. She's going to stay in New York and organize things here. He set his papers aside and jumped when his phone rang. He certainly hadn't expected his mother to call. "What's up?" he asked.

"Talking might be easier," his mother said with a slight huff. "Are you going to need an assistant here? Because I'm not going to organize your life for you. That's too much work for an old lady like me."

"You're not old. Marjorie's handling finding an assistant for me." He was so danged tired and not into having this conversation. Marjorie would find him someone he could work well with. It wasn't like he needed someone to work as many hours as she did. He'd still have her to maintain his master calendar and handle the bulk of his needs. Having someone local was a good idea, though.

"Thelma Wilson's grandson just graduated from college and is looking for a job. I told her you were coming and would probably need someone, so I said I'd pass it along."

Great. Just what he needed. His mother trying to find his assistant for him. Thomas was about to tell her that Marjorie would find who he needed, but he wasn't in the mood to argue with his mother. It would get him nowhere and then his mother would be upset. "Have him send his résumé and things to HR in New York. They're handling everything for me." There, that was pretty painless.

"Okay. I'll pass that on to Thelma. Can you tell me the email address he should use?" she asked, and Thomas relayed it. "You travel safe, and call your father and me when you get in." He heard the excitement in her voice. Thomas hadn't been home as much as he probably should have been in the last few years. She and his dad had been delighted when he'd told them he was moving home.

"I will, Mom. You and Dad take it easy, and I'll see you on Wednesday." He got in late on Tuesday and didn't want to disturb them. "Maybe we can have dinner if you and Dad are free." It was time he slowed down and took the chance to try to build a life that didn't revolve around work.

"There are some nice young men in town, who like other men, and…."

He groaned. Before he came out to his parents, his mother had done her best to fix him up with every eligible girl she knew. Back then he'd made himself busy so he wouldn't have to go on those dates. "Mom, I'm coming home to spend some time with you and Dad. I'm still going to be busy." And the last thing he wanted was his mother picking out men for him. Yes, he was pleased that his parents accepted him for who he was, but his mom playing gay matchmaker was a little over the line. "If I want to date, I will. I'm not some troll who needs his mom to get him dates."

"You be nice," she scolded.

"Then you put away your matchmaking skills and let my love life be." He sighed, because no matter how many times he scolded her, his mother was his mother and was going to do exactly what she liked. "Mess in Collin's love life. He's the straight one, and he's single again." For, like, the third time. She could matchmake with him all she wanted. Lord knew he needed it. "Or better yet, leave us both to figure out our own love lives."

His mom was quiet, and Thomas knew instantly that something was up. "I introduced him to Karla," she confessed sheepishly.

"*You* did that!" he gasped.

"He married her!" Mom protested. "All I did was introduce them. I had no idea she'd turn out to be such a harpy. She was nice when I met her and invited her to dinner."

He rolled his eyes even though she couldn't see it. "That only goes to show that you make a lousy matchmaker. You're too danged nice and you see the good in everyone. I knew that woman was the spawn of Satan two seconds after I met her, but by then she already had that damn ring on her finger and her claws so deep into Collin, it was sickening. All she ever wanted was Collin's money… or what she thought she could extract from me through Collin."

It damn near ruined his relationship with his brother. Karla demanded things—jewelry, a new home—and Collin would try to get them for her. Then, when he couldn't afford it, Collin came to Thomas for money, hat in hand, feeling like a loser. Eventually Thomas stopped the handouts. Collin didn't speak to him for months… until Karla finally left and Collin was out from under her influence. Then and only then did the old Collin start to return.

"I am not a lousy matchmaker. I only make introductions. All I did was invite her to dinner one night. Your brother did the rest." She was getting huffy.

"Still, you have to take some responsibility." If he could get his mother to back off, then he would be in good shape. "Let Collin and me be. We can find partners just fine on our own."

"Fine." She huffed, and Thomas knew she wasn't giving up, only doing a strategic retreat. His matchmaking mother would be back soon enough. "Then should I uninvite the people I have coming over for dinner tonight?"

"Mom. Collin just got divorced three months ago. Let him breathe." For Pete's sake, she moved fast.

"If he doesn't get married to a nice girl soon, they're going to be too old to have kids and I'm never going to be a grandmother." Now the sniffles began, which Thomas knew was his total weakness as far as she was concerned.

"Fine. I'm staying out of this. But if Collin marries another harpy like Karla, I'm holding you responsible." He chuckled when his mother sputtered on the other end of the line. "I'm going to go. You and Dad have a good night." He was about to hang up but paused. "And to say it again, don't you try to fix me up with anyone."

He ended the call, wondering if his mother would listen at all or not. Either way, he was not going to fall for anyone his mother tried to set him up with. He loved her to death, but the woman had bad taste in potential daughters-in-law. Thomas could only imagine the kind of men she'd try to pick out for him. Hell, he'd end up married to his father. The thought made him shudder as he put his phone on the coffee table.

Thomas returned his attention to the papers he'd brought home with him, but quickly realized he was getting nothing done. Setting those things aside, he decided to get some of his personal things packed for the move. Most of the things, he didn't really care about and the movers could take care of. But there were things he didn't want strangers pawing through, so he pulled the suitcases out from under the bed, laid them out, and began filling them with underwear and the clothes he was going to want to take with him on the plane.

He paused at a knock at the door and went to open it.

Blaze breezed into the apartment, looking around. "For God's sake, let me guess—you're packing." He put his hands on his hips, glaring at Thomas. "It's a Friday night, the last one you're going to spend in New York for a while." Blaze peered into the bedroom and then back at him. "I knew I had to come save you from yourself. Go back in there and put on some decent clothes. You and I are going out, and we're going to find you some young, hot guy. You might as well leave town with a bang."

"Your puns are awful," Thomas said. "I'm tired, and I have a big day tomorrow."

Blaze shook his head. "You're going to stand around, watching the movers pack, making sure they don't put a finger through the de Kooning or the Pollock. Other than that, you'll sit on the sofa working. So who cares?" He waited for Thomas's answer, and when he didn't have a good one, Thomas went into the bedroom to change.

"Why are you my friend again?" Thomas asked as he looked through his closet.

"That's easy. Because I'm the only person who won't let you sit around and wallow in your own crapulence on a Friday night." Blaze's voice drifted in from the other room. "Put on something hot, and make sure the pants are tight enough to show off your ass."

"Jesus, Blaze. I'm not twenty years old anymore. I don't need to do all that crap." Thomas grabbed a pair of comfortable jeans and tossed them on the bed, then went looking for a silk shirt he liked.

"We're damn near forty. We need to do all that crap and more. Have you looked in the mirror lately? Neither of us is fat, but we're spreading nonetheless. Our asses are wider and our legs thicker. We can't wear those skinny jeans we used to pour ourselves into when we were young. So now we have to show off the goods and remind the boys that with a little time comes a whole lot of experience."

Blaze always looked good, and Thomas had never noticed any spreading where his friend was concerned.

Thomas finished dressing and came out. "How is this, your highness?" He smirked.

"Good God. We're going out for the evening, to a club, not to a cotillion." Blaze brushed past him and went right to Thomas's closet. "Put this on, and those jeans look like you got them at Old Farts R Us." He dug through and tossed a pair of black jeans on the bed. "Put those on. Black is slimming."

"But that shirt is too small."

"Perfect. It should be tight to show off your arms." Blaze stepped out of the room, and Thomas wondered if this was worth it.

He changed clothes again. The jeans hugged his hips and waist so tightly that they were a second skin, and the shirt stretched over his chest. When he looked in the full-length mirror, he had to admit that he looked pretty good.

"All right. Let's go," Thomas said, emerging from the bedroom. Blaze nodded and turned toward the door. Thomas got his wallet and keys, followed Blaze out, and locked the apartment door. After taking the elevator down to the first floor, they were greeted by the doorman and then stepped out into the Upper West Side night air.

"I can't believe you're giving all this up," Blaze said as he hailed a cab. "What kind of place are you going to have in Colorado Springs?"

Thomas shrugged. "I don't know yet. I haven't bought a house. I figured I'd rent a place for a while and then move when I found somewhere I really liked." He wasn't dumb enough to buy anything sight unseen.

"You're moving pretty quickly with this whole thing." Blaze looked up and down the street, and they walked the block or so toward Fifth.

"Collin called a few weeks ago, and he said Mom and Dad were having a tougher time of it. They would never say anything, but mom's rheumatism is making it harder for her to get around, and Dad is having to do more and more for her. Collin helps, but he works strange hours at the restaurant, and, well…." Thomas shrugged. "I'm nearly forty and I'm tired." He stepped around a pile of dog leavings, wishing the offending owner had been given a huge ticket. "I've been working night and day to get this business started and then to make it successful. Now I want the chance to spend some time with my mom and dad before it's too late."

Blaze reached the corner, whistling shrilly for a cab. "The last thing I would ever think of is moving home to see my parents. God, I'd rather lose a leg than spend an hour back in Georgia with my father. The man is a fanatic. He turned his back on me as soon as he thought I might be gay." When a cab pulled to the curb, Blaze pulled open the back door to climb in, and Thomas got in as well. He should have called his limousine service and arranged a ride. That was, if Blaze had given him any kind of notice at all, like a normal person.

"The Brick," Blaze told the driver, who nodded, taking off.

"You really want to go there?" That gay club had been around for decades.

"It's been completely remodeled and is trendy again. Guys are done with that techno shit and want some good, clean… well, maybe more like hot and dirty action. This is the place where all the hot guys are right now." And Blaze would know. His gift was to keep up with what was gay, hot, and where his money could get him anything he wanted.

Thomas turned to Blaze. "Have you ever given any thought to settling down?"

Blaze's eyes burned in the semidarkness and flashing lights as the blocks passed. "Yeah, I did the whole relationship thing. Remember Mathias? He was…." Blaze seemed at a loss for words. "You know how well that all worked out." He shook his head. "I'm way better off without all those awful entanglements that only leave you wishing to hell that you hadn't let him in your heart… or your apartment." Blaze swore under his breath. "The bastard stole me blind, and I needed a course of penicillin to fully eradicate him. So, no, I haven't thought about settling down any time soon. I'll cruise the boys until I'm too ugly and old. And then just hire them."

Thomas knew the whole story about Mathias, but he hadn't fully realized how deeply the little shit had hurt Blaze. Which pissed Thomas off, because he should have been paying closer attention. He thought about trying to find Mathias just so he could teach the stupid piece of crap a lesson about messing with people. "You can't let one asshole dictate your outlook like that."

They pulled into Midtown, and Blaze turned toward the window. "Bullshit. I've been out with other guys, and things always end the same damn way." He didn't even look at Thomas as he spoke, but Thomas could hear the pain in his voice. "I have good friends that I can trust, and I go to clubs or bars when I want someone to warm my bed for a night." He finally shifted to look at Thomas again. "I always thought you felt the same way. I mean, you never dated anyone, not seriously."

"I never dated anyone… well, with the exception of Angus." Thomas rolled his eyes. The few times he had gone out with a guy more than once, something at work would come up and he'd end up cutting the date short or canceling. The guys got the message pretty quickly that his job came first and they were going to be a distant second. There were never any third dates—except for Angus, and that had turned into a total disaster… for both of them. "Not really."

"See, I figured you got hurt by some shithead and never told me."

"Nope. Just never had time." Thomas turned, looking out the window as the neighborhood changed from apartment buildings to clubs and businesses.

"Do you want a social life?" Blaze asked as the cab pulled over.

Thomas opened the door, thankful to be able to evade the question. He paid the driver and joined Blaze as the cab sped away from the curb.

"You didn't answer my question."

Thomas gazed at the line of guys waiting to get into the club. This was a bad idea. It was going to take hours for them to get inside, and the last thing he wanted to be doing was waiting in a fucking line on a Friday night. "I think I might. I don't know." He knew he was getting tired of spending his days at the office and his nights doing more work. "There has to be more to life than just this." He waved a hand in front of him, not really referring to the club, but things in general.

"No need to worry, my friend." Blaze walked up to the doorman, spoke to him for a few seconds, and then motioned. The velvet rope lifted out of their way, and they were inside, just like that.

Thomas didn't have time to think about it. Instantly he was surrounded by the throbbing beat of the music and the crush of men, many of them shirtless, ripped chests and bellies covered in a glistening sheen of sweat—beauty and sex on display everywhere he looked.

"Where do you want to start?" Blaze asked as a man sauntered right up to him. He was shorter—a pocket powerhouse, judging by all the muscles. He stood on his tiptoes and whispered something to Blaze before sliding his arm around Blaze's waist. Blaze smiled and made his way to the bar, while Thomas looked around once again, feeling like a junior high kid left standing by the wall while all the others danced.

Thomas, as the head of a very successful company built from the ground up, should be able to go out there and talk to guys. There wasn't anything to it. He talked to people all day long with no problem whatsoever. But right now, all the guys were gorgeous, tanned, toned… hot.

"Go on out there and meet people," Blaze said, pressing a beer glass into his hand before downing his shot and turning away with short-and-studly. They made their way to the dance floor, where Blaze smoothly took the other man in his arms and they burned it up. Even Thomas could see they were hot together, and he had been told on multiple occasions that he was pretty clueless about things like that. His own dance moves lay somewhere between a dying chicken and a scarecrow.

Thomas slowly approached the bar and found an empty place to watch what was happening. He finished his beer and ordered another one.

"Hey," said a man, about thirty, with jet-black hair and piercing eyes, as he leaned over the bar, glancing at Thomas.

"Hello," Thomas said, giving him his best smile. Why was he so nervous? Thomas quickly searched for something to say that didn't sound like a line. "Would you like a drink?"

"That would be nice, thanks." The guy settled next to him, smiling as Thomas got the bartender's attention and ordered a martini. "I've never been here before." He turned back to the dance floor, and Thomas followed his gaze. "I had no idea there would be so many older guys trolling for young dudes." The martini arrived, and then the guy was gone.

Thomas shook his head and paid for the drink. Being shot down before he even took a chance was one thing, but the guy being rude was dispiriting. If men were like that, Thomas didn't understand why anyone bothered at all.

He turned in his seat to watch as Blaze and Studly melded themselves together, dancing, or fucking standing up—it was hard to tell which. He ordered another drink and waited to see if there was anyone to try to talk with.

Thomas quickly realized this whole thing was a mistake. It only helped to drive the point home that he needed a change. Thomas threaded through the crowd to Blaze, explained that he was going home, and told him to have fun. Then he weaved out through the crush of bodies and into the night air. This time he called his car service, requested a limo, and waited, watching the boys in line. When the car pulled up, he got inside, ignoring the looks of curiosity, and rode home.

It was definitely time to get out of New York.

ANDREW GREY is the author of nearly 100 works of Contemporary Gay Romantic fiction. After twenty-seven years in corporate America, he has now settled down in Central Pennsylvania with his husband, Dominic, and his laptop. An interesting ménage. Andrew grew up in western Michigan with a father who loved to tell stories and a mother who loved to read them. Since then he has lived throughout the country and traveled throughout the world. He is a recipient of the RWA Centennial Award, has a master's degree from the University of Wisconsin–Milwaukee, and now writes full-time. Andrew's hobbies include collecting antiques, gardening, and leaving his dirty dishes anywhere but in the sink (particularly when writing). He considers himself blessed with an accepting family, fantastic friends, and the world's most supportive and loving partner. Andrew currently lives in beautiful, historic Carlisle, Pennsylvania.

Email: andrewgrey@comcast.net

Website: www.andrewgreybooks.com

FIRE
AND
ANDREW GREY
CARLISLE COPS
1

Carlisle Cops: Book One

Officer Red Markham knows about the ugly side of life after a car accident left him scarred and his parents dead. His job policing the streets of Carlisle, PA, only adds to the ugliness, and lately, drug overdoses have been on the rise. One afternoon, Red is dispatched to the local Y for a drowning accident involving a child. Arriving on site, he finds the boy rescued by lifeguard Terry Baumgartner. Of course, Red isn't surprised when gorgeous Terry won't give him and his ugly mug the time of day.

Overhearing one of the officers comment about him being shallow opens Terry's eyes. Maybe he isn't as kindhearted as he always thought. His friend Julie suggests he help those less fortunate by delivering food to the elderly. On his route he meets outspoken Margie, a woman who says what's on her mind. Turns out, she's Officer Red's aunt.

Red's and Terry's worlds collide as Red tries to track the source of the drugs and protect Terry from an ex-boyfriend who won't take no for an answer. Together they might discover a chance for more than they expected—if they can see beyond what's on the surface.

www. dreamspinnerpress.com

ANDREW GREY
CARLISLE
COPS
2

Carlisle Cops: Book Two

Carter Schunk is a dedicated police officer with a difficult past and a big heart. When he's called to a domestic disturbance, he finds a fatally injured woman, and a child, Alex, who is in desperate need of care. Child Services is called, and the last man on earth Carter wants to see walks through the door. Carter had a fling with Donald a year ago and found him as cold as ice since it ended.

Donald (Ice) Ickle has had a hard life he shares with no one, and he's closed his heart to all. It's partly to keep himself from getting hurt and partly the way he deals with a job he's good at, because he does what needs to be done without getting emotionally involved. When he meets Carter again, he maintains his usual distance, but Carter gets under his skin, and against his better judgment, Donald lets Carter guilt him into taking Alex when there isn't other foster care available. Carter even offers to help care for the boy.

Donald has a past he doesn't want to discuss with anyone, least of all Carter, who has his own past he'd just as soon keep to himself. But it's Alex's secrets that could either pull them together or rip them apart—secrets the boy isn't able to tell them and yet could be the key to happiness for all of them.

www. dreamspinnerpress.com

FIRE AND RAIN
ANDREW GREY
CARLISLE COPS
3

Carlisle Cops: Book Three

Since the death of their mother, Josten Applewhite has done what he's had to do to take care of his little brother and keep their small family together. But in an instant, a stroke of bad luck tears down what little home he's managed to build, and Jos and Isaac end up on the streets.

That's where Officer Kip Rogers finds them, and even though he knows he should let the proper authorities handle things, he cannot find it in his heart to turn them away, going so far as to invite them to stay in his home until they get back on their feet. With the help of Kip and his friends, Jos starts to rebuild his life. But experience has taught him nothing comes for free, and the generosity seems too good to be true—just like everything about Kip.

Kip's falling hard for Jos, and he likes the way Jos and Isaac make his big house feel like a home. But their arrangement can't be permanent, not with Jos set on making his own way. Then a distant relative emerges, determined to destroy Jos's family, and Kip knows Jos needs him—even if he's not ready to admit it.

www. dreamspinnerpress.com

ANDREW GREY
CARLISLE COPS
4

Carlisle Cops: Book Four

Fisher Moreland has been cast out of his family because they can no longer deal with his issues. Fisher is bipolar and living day to day, trying to manage his condition, but he hasn't always had much control over his life and has self-medicated with whatever he could find.

JD Burnside has been cut off from his family because of a scandal back home. He moved to Carlisle but brought his Southern charm and warmth along with him. When he sees Fisher on a park bench on a winter's night, he invites Fisher to join him and his friends for a late-night meal.

At first Fisher doesn't know what to make of JD, but he slowly comes out of his shell. And when Fisher's job is threatened because of a fire, JD's support and care is more than Fisher ever thought he could expect. But when people from Fisher's past turn up in town at the center of a resurgent drug epidemic, Fisher knows they could very well sabotage his budding relationship with JD.

www. dreamspinnerpress.com

ANDREW GREY
CARLISLE COPS
5

Carlisle Cops: Book Five

Brock Ferguson knew he might run into his ex-boyfriend, Vincent Geraldini, when he took his first job as a police officer in Carlisle. Vincent's attitude during a routine traffic stop reminds Brock why their relationship didn't last.

What Brock doesn't expect is finding two scared children in the trunk of a Corvette. He's also surprised to learn the kids' mother is Vincent's sister. But his immediate concern is the safety of the two children, Abey and Penny, and he offers to comfort and care for them when their mother is taken into custody.

Vincent is also shocked to learn what his sister has done. For the sake of the kids, he and Brock bury the hatchet—and soon find they have much more in common than they realized. With Abey and Penny's help, they grow closer, until the four of them start to feel like a family. But Vincent's sister and her boyfriend—an equal-opportunity jerk—could tear down everything they're trying to build.

www. dreamspinnerpress.com

ANDREW GREY
CARLISLE
COPS
6

Carlisle Cops: Book Six

Carlisle police officer Dwayne knows what Robin is doing the moment he lays eyes on the young man at Bronco's club. But he doesn't know that, like him, Robin also comes from a family who cast him out for being gay, or that he's still lugging around the pain of that rejection. Robin leaves the club, and soon after Dwayne decides to as well—and is close by when things between Robin and his client turn violent.

When Dwayne finds out Robin is the victim of a scam that lost him his apartment, he can't leave Robin to fend for himself on the streets. Despite Dwayne's offer of help and even opening up his home, it's hard for Robin to trust anything good. The friendship between them grows, and just as the two men start warming up to each other, Robin's sister passes away, naming Robin to care for her son. Worse yet, their pasts creep back in to tear down the family and sense of belonging both of them long for.

Will their fledgling romance dissipate like fog in the sun before it has a chance to burn bright?

www. dreamspinnerpress.com

FOR
MORE
OF THE
BEST
GAY
ROMANCE
DREAMSPINNER
PRESS
dreamspinnerpress.com